SPIRIT OF THE WOLF

Yano's Adventures

Volume 2

RANDY HOGUE

For information contact: info@outlawspublishing.com
Cover Art by Randy Hogue
Cover design by Outlaws Publishing.
Published by Outlaws Publishing.
September 2024
10 9 8 7 6 5 4 3 2 1

"The Best and Most Beautiful
things in the world cannot
be seen or even touched
they must be felt with the heart"
        ______Helen Keller

FORWORD:

The Adventures of Yano, the first-born son of the Adams' family, brings excitement, joy and fear to a young boy, at the tender age of ten.

Skilled and adventurous, Yano believed he was ready for the journey to manhood, but could he survive the danger of the wilderness in the Appalachian Mountains, alone with Bobcats, Mountain Lions, and Bears nearby. The journey unfolds as treasure and trouble intermingle with the Spirit of the Wolf.

A grave danger was lurking near their home for his younger sister, Ayita that ultimately left the family with heart wrenching fear for her safety and return. Where is she, what is happening to her? An unthinkable tragedy for any family.

How far would you go to save a loved one?

CHAPTER I

On a cold October morning, Alan Adams stood at the train station in Shepherd Springs, Virginia waiting for the train to take him to Rockford, Virginia. Mr. Stockburn needed Alan desperately to oversee the operations of the new coal mine opening soon. It was a hard decision for Alan, he wanted to help Mr. Stockburn, but he also didn't want to uproot his family from the home and mountains they loved so much. Mr. Stockburn knew what a hard decision this was for Alan, so he came up with a plan he thought just might work for them both.

The plan was for Alan to take the early morning train to Rockford each Monday, be at the mines for three days, and return home to Shepherd Springs. Since the mines in Shepherd Springs had not completely shut down, Alan and John Thomas would share the superintendent's duties for both mines. Once the last mine in Shepherd Springs shut down, they would split shifts at the Rockford mines. After listening to the plan, Alan knew this would work out great for him and his family. He promised Mr. Stockburn to be with him at least two more years and maybe more. He felt this was a way to show his appreciation to Mr. Stockburn for hiring him twelve years earlier and for making it possible for him to take the position at the new mine without moving his family,

Some of the miners had already relocated to Rockford and helped build the shanties needed for living quarters. There were a few still in Shepherd Springs that stayed behind to work the last mine until it closed, and they too would soon move to Rockford. The setup at the new site was much like the one in Shepherd Springs. The town of Rockford was a little smaller, but was expected to boom when coal mining started.

Alan's good friend and neighbor, Jacob Bolin and wife Sarah, had already moved into one of the shanties. Jacob excelled in the mining business and John promoted him to the new Safety Officer for the Rockford mines upon Alan's recommendation.

Yano, Alan and Odina's oldest son, was now eleven years old and very mature and responsible for a young man his age. When Alan left for Rockford, he knew Yano would help his mother with the household duties and handle anything that happened while he was away. All the children had chores, and Yano set a great example for them to follow. He was teaching the seven-year-old twins, Koda and Ayita, along with their five-year-old baby sister, Nokomis, survival skills.

At such a young age, Yano had become a very good hunter and fisherman. He hunted mainly with a bow and arrow his father made for him and helped supply food for the family by harvesting deer, squirrels, rabbits and grouse. Although he was taught how to use a gun, and the rules of gun safety, he preferred the bow. His love of exploring sometimes would take him over one mountain after another just to see what was on the other side. This curiosity would often make him extremely late getting home, causing his mother to be very concerned and worried for his safety, she knew the dangers of the mountains.

CHAPTER 2

When Yano was ten years old, he thought he was a man already. He told his father he knew how to survive in the wilderness by himself if he had to. Alan knew he had taught his son well and he always told him how proud he was of him, he was a good hunter and fisherman, he had no doubt he could survive, however, there was a test he must pass to prove he was ready to enter manhood. Yano was excited to take the test, so his father said, when he was sure he was ready, he would explain the rules. A very confident ten-year-old said he was ready without even knowing what the test would be, until later.

Alan talked with Odina and told her he was taking Yano up in the mountains tonight to give him the test of manhood. She knew what the test was and was overflowing with emotion knowing her first-born son was beginning the journey into manhood.

After supper, Alan told Yano to put a jacket on, take his knife and come with him. As they started walking into the mountains, they had to use the light of the moon to guide their way. Yano had a puzzled look on his face, not feeling as confident as he did earlier when Alan told him it was time to start the test. When they approached the waterfall, he told Yano this would be where the test began, just sit on the stump here and listen to me. He then took out a piece of cloth and blindfolded Yano, so he could not see. He must sit on the stump all night without removing the blindfold even if he heard noises, and he would be back in the morning. The rules were; he could only remove the blindfold when daylight came, and he could hear the birds chirping. This would prove he was ready to start the journey into manhood by showing this act of bravery. Yano, hearing his father walk away, now realized he was all alone in the mountains until his father came back after daylight. If only he could just fall asleep until morning, but sleep did not come. He heard animal sounds; leaves rustling and sounds he had never heard before. It felt like he had been sitting on the stump for two days. With every sound, he thought it could be a bear or mountain lion about to attack, but he didn't remove the blindfold. The night dragged on forever, but then he heard the howling of a Wolf. He had never heard a Wolf howling, but he knew it was a Wolf from stories he had heard growing up. Too frightened to sleep, he sat without moving, until morning finally came, and he could see the morning light through the blindfold. He heard the birds chirping, the time had come to remove the blindfold. Yano was shivering from the cold mountain morning, but feeling enormously proud of himself as he removed the blindfold and tried to focus his eyes on his surroundings. After sitting on the stump all night, his legs were stiff as he stood up. He first looked to see what was behind him and to his amazement, he could see the man that left him in the mountains, sitting on the ground about twenty feet behind him with a smile on his face from ear to ear. His father, unbeknown to Yano, had sat there all night keeping a watchful eye on his brave young son. He wanted Yano to know how proud of him he was, but cautioned him that he could not tell his siblings or anyone about the experience. That was his first test, but there would be many more during the journey into manhood, some more difficult situations than others, and his skills, training and experiences would give him the necessary tools to handle those situations on his journey as they came along.

Yano told his father about hearing the howling of the Wolf during the night, he wasn't frightened, instead he felt a sense of calm as the mountains became silent during the howling of the Wolf. Alan told him the elders always said that treasures could be found at the location of the howling Wolf, but treasure could mean many things. It was time to go home now and have breakfast. Yano was happy and ready; he was hungry and sleepy, but he knew he must complete his chores before taking a nap. As any father would be, Alan was pleased he understood his responsibilities in caring for the livestock before he gave in to his need for food and sleep, another sign he was well on his way to manhood.

While on the walk home, he asked his father what he thought the treasure was at the location of the howling of the Wolf. It could mean danger was close and the Wolf scared it away or it may mean your treasure was twenty feet behind you all night long providing protection. Yet, it could be possible the treasure was twenty feet in front of me, allowing me to witness the bravery of my young son.

Now, Yano understood more about what a treasure could be and how each one could have a different meaning. Smiling he looked up, thankful to the man he called father that walked beside him.

Arriving back at the cabin, Odina had breakfast ready and waiting for them.

CHAPTER 3

It had been over a year since Alan had heard from his very first friend Sloppy. Months before he was to start making trips to Rockford, he told Odina he was concerned about not hearing from Sloppy for so long. He knew the man could take care of himself, but he could sense something wasn't right. Alan told Odina he would take Yano, and the mule loaded with supplies and try to find him and his cabin. It would probably take two days to get there, but he felt sure he could find him from what Sloppy told him. He had taken two weeks off from work at the coal mines to catch up on chores at home, but finding Sloppy was more important, maybe he could get some of the chores caught up before he left.

Odina said, "We will be fine while you're gone, and if we need help, we can always count on the Bolins, just be careful and find him."

They had no idea of Sloppy's age, but he would be ten years older from when they first met. He had been living the mountain man life for forty years.

The next morning, Alan and Yano headed out pulling their pack mule loaded down with supplies behind them in hopes of finding Sloppy. He had never been to Sloppy's place, but he remembered the day Sloppy told him what signs to look for and how to find him. Alan was a good tracker and at eleven years old, so was Yano.

Travel was slow, the terrain was rough, but he had located the two stacks of rocks Sloppy described. He remembered Sloppy saying, "If you find the two stacks of rocks, go between them and up the draw to the right. If you don't go between them and wind up going up another draw, you will never find me. You are still a long way from my cabin when you reach the two stacks of rocks, but if you are as good a tracker, as I think you are, you'll find me." They planned to go a little further before setting up camp for the night since Alan could see some signs of where Sloppy had traveled in the past, but there were no fresh signs. As dark approached, they set up camp.

At daybreak the next morning, they loaded up and continued their search. After a few hours of traveling slowly, Alan noticed a draw that went to the left that had some old signs showing where horses may had traveled probably some months before, he just knew it would lead to Sloppy's cabin. Going up the draw between steep mountains was a narrow trail that ran beside a creek, he knew Sloppy would be close to water and was sure they were going the right way. The trail and creek made a sharp bend to the right, and he could tell the land seemed to flatten out some, then he spotted a cabin about a hundred yards ahead. Slowly approaching the cabin, Alan called out to Sloppy, but he received no response. As they got closer, he spotted Sloppy's horse and mule in the coral looking poorly. Still calling out Sloppy's name as he approached the cabin, still no response. Alan opened the door to the cabin, not knowing what he would find. It was cold inside the cabin with no sign or odor of cooked food. The only odor he could smell was that of human waste. Over in the corner was a bed with bear pelts spread out on top of it. As he approached the bed, he lifted the bear pelts back to find Sloppy lying under them. He was alive, but just barely, He was breathing, but couldn't speak or at least not where he could be heard.

Sloppy opened his eyes, and tried to speak, but he did not have enough air to make a sound.

~~~~~~

Sloppy had an old wood burning stove in the cabin, so Alan told Yano to build a fire in it, then get some of the Ginseng roots they brought, so he could make some Ginseng tea. Sloppy had soiled the bed so bad and had probably been laying there for days or even months. He looked like he had lost a lot of weight and had a rattling noise in his chest like he probably had pneumonia. Alan was so glad he brought Yano with him because together they were going to do whatever they could to save his friend's life. He wished Dr. Hogue was there, but he wasn't, so he would have to do what he had seen Dr. Hogue do when Clyde Bolin had pneumonia. Upon further inspection of his friend, he saw he had a broken leg, he had wrapped it up himself, then laid in bed unable to get up and fix something to eat or build a fire for warmth. Alan was so angry at himself for not coming a month or two earlier.

After cleaning his friend up, he removed the soiled pelts and bed linens from the bed and told Yano to feed
~~~~~~

Sloppy's horse and mule some sweet feed they had brought and then to take care of their horses and put them in the coral with Sloppy's. Alan knew he could not leave him there like that, so he would try to get him well enough to travel by horseback or sled. The cabin was warm, and Alan was able to get Sloppy to sip on some Ginseng tea while he cleaned his broken leg and put a fresh splint on it. He remembered seeing Dr. Hogue tapping Clyde's back when he had pneumonia, so he did the same thing to Sloppy.

Alan had a lot of thinking to do, he had to get Sloppy home, where he could look after him and Dr. Hogue could treat him, but two days of rough traveling at this point might kill him. He was able to get Sloppy to drink more Ginseng tea and take a small bite of cured ham they brought with them. Yano had been busy taking care of the horses and mule along with gathering firewood. In a couple more hours he would do the tapping therapy on Sloppy's back to help break loose the mucus in his lungs. They had brought enough food to last about a week or more, but he would get Yano to go out tomorrow morning and see if he could harvest squirrels, rabbits or grouse to eat. He also needed to get Sloppy's horse and mule healthy enough to make the trip too, he couldn't leave them behind. Alan and Yano ate, then brought in enough wood for the fireplace and cook stove. One more therapy session for Sloppy, then they all went to sleep.

When morning came, Alan made a pot of coffee, heated up a few of the biscuits Odina made for them and helped Sloppy take a few sips of coffee along with a few bites of ham and biscuit. Sloppy could talk more now with a little volume, but was still too weak to travel.

Yano went out hunting with his bow and arrow, that he was very good with and was able to harvest a grouse. He was happy to explore new territory, he got his excitement of exploring from his father.

Alan got Sloppy to sit up in a chair for about an hour, while drinking a little more coffee. It was amazing how quick a few bites of food and some Ginseng tea along with coffee perked him up. He had already gained some of his strength back, but Alan knew it would take a while. Alan thought Sloppy felt well enough to speak, so he asked him how he broke his leg.

Sloppy motioned for Alan to come closer, because he still had no volume in his voice. "I was using a rope to come down a very steep rock face cliff, when my hands gave out causing me to slip and fall about forty feet to the bottom. On the way down my foot got caught between two rocks and my body weight still falling caused my leg to snap then pull out from the rocks. When I hit the ground, I must have hit my head on something and was knocked out." Sloppy said he wasn't sure how long he laid there unconscious, it could have been a day or two or could have been a week. He said it was mid-day when he fell and early morning when he came to, he was awakened by hearing the howling of a Wolf that sounded like it was on top of the rock cliff above him, he knew then he was alive, and the Wolf was his protector.

Alan's eyes got really big when he heard Sloppy say that because that was how Sloppy found his best friend Fred Smith years ago. The location of the howling Wolf was where he found Fred. Sloppy said he had to crawl and hop about a half mile to get back to his cabin. He knew he had to try and set the broken bone in his leg in place, so he tied his foot to the footboard on his bed and pushed himself backwards. The pain from that caused him to pass out and when he came to, he wrapped his leg, best he could to keep the bone set without moving. Sloppy said he didn't remember getting up again until Alan found him.

Alan apologized for not coming sooner, he knew something wasn't right, when he had not seen him for so long.

Sloppy told him, "No need to apologize, Alan, I have stayed in these mountains for a long time without coming out for supplies many times before. You didn't know, but I'm glad you came when you did and I'm also glad that you are a good tracker. I will be forever in your debt for what you have done for me."

Alan said, "I'm not done yet, I want to take you, your horse and mule back home with us to take care of you, until you are well enough to return here to the mountain life you love."

Alan and Yano had been gone from home six days now and he knew Odina was getting worried, so they needed to talk about taking Sloppy and his animals back pretty soon.

Sloppy was eating better, talking better and even moving around a little in the cabin with the help of the crutches Alan made for him. Alan had been doing the therapy, tapping twice a day to help with Sloppy's pneumonia, but he needed a doctor's care. Sloppy asked Alan to do him another favor before they packed up to go home. He told Alan there was a long rope still hanging down from the top of the cliff where he fell, and he didn't want it left there. Alan was pretty sure why he didn't want the rope left there for someone else to find, but it would be up to Sloppy to tell him. Alan asked where the place was. Sloppy said, "about half a mile down the trail, y'all came in on, there's a tree shaped like a chair in between the trail and creek. Indians would bend sapling trees into shapes, so they would grow into different shapes. They would do that to mark a place of interest. Sloppy said, I bent this one probably thirty years ago."

Yano spoke up and said, "I saw that tree when coming here."

Sloppy then said, go to your right at the chair tree, cross the creek, go to the top of a small hill and find rocks stacked about two feet high. Then in a straight line from the chair tree to the stacked rocks to the rock cliff is where the rope will be found. Sloppy then told them, "You don't have to go to the top of the rock cliff, you can retrieve the rope from the bottom because of the way I tied the rope. I wrapped it around a tree at the top, then tied both ends together and threw it over the cliff to the bottom. When I got to the bottom, all I had to do was untie the end and pull the rope down.

Alan asked Yano if he thought he could find the place and get the rope.

Yano said, "I'll find it, I remember where the chair tree was."

Alan told Yano this would be another test for his journey to manhood, he was proud of his eleven-year-old son's confidence.

Sloppy told Yano to stay alert for mountain lions; they frequent the rock cliffs.

Alan gave Yano his Colt 44 caliber pistol for protection should he need it.

Sloppy said, "you will need to tie Smokie to a tree near the chair tree and walk the rest of the way."

Yano saddled up and left. When he got to the chair tree, he tied Smokie to a tree and started walking up the little hill that Sloppy described. Once on top, he found the stack of rocks. He could still see the chair tree, so he drew an imaginary straight line to the cliffs and walked that way. He went right to the rope and while he was untying the end, he looked up and saw what looked like a hat about twenty feet up. He used the rope to climb the twenty feet and retrieved what he knew was Sloppy's hat. As he repelled back down, he heard the most hair-raising sound of a mountain lion screaming and saw it about thirty feet above him. Holding on to the rope with one hand, he pulled the pistol from the holster and fired at the big cat. He missed the cat, but hit a rock beside it and that was enough to scare it away. Yano's heart was racing, but he finished the task and returned to the cabin with the rope and Sloppy's hat.

Sloppy was pleased to have his hat and the rope retrieved. He never did say, but Alan knew he didn't want some stranger to come by the rope hanging there, and snoop around that area. Sloppy and Fred Smith were the best of friends and did a lot of things the same way. Alan thought that Sloppy and Fred had discussed how and where to hide their treasures.

Chapter 5

The morning had come to leave Sloppy's cabin and take him home with them to try and get him well. Alan had built a drag sled for Sloppy to lay on, strapped to Alan's mule. They would walk Sloppy's horse and mule, since both were still too weak to carry any weight. The trail was rough, and they had to go slow with many stops to check on Sloppy. After traveling about halfway home, they stopped and made camp. Alan laid out some of the pelts they brought and made Sloppy a bed close to the fire. Yano tended to the livestock and gave them some oats and sweet feed they had brought with them. After, they had some grub and coffee, Alan and Yano laid out their bedrolls close to the fire. Alan and Sloppy were talking while waiting for sleep to come. Alan said, "Sloppy, how old are you? I've known you for ten years and don't know how old you are."

"Guess," said Sloppy."

To Alan, he looked about ninety, but he just said, "I really don't know."

"Well, I left the coal mining life, the sawmill life, and the small-town life and went deep into the Appalachian Mountains to be a mountain man when I was twenty-eight years old. That's been my life for forty years, so that makes me sixty-eight years old now, I think. Living life in the mountains, one does not remember much about days, months or years, but knows the seasons. God and the wilderness will always show you the seasons. In the winter, the trees will shed their leaves, the temperature can be bitterly cold, snow will fall from the sky, ice will form where there's moisture and most days are gray and cool. In the spring, plants come to life, leaves reappear on the trees, birds will be chirping, temperatures will warm up, beautiful colors of wildflowers will warm your soul and one starts to feel more alive in the springtime. The summers in the mountains are usually my least favorite, but you must go through one to get to another. The temperatures can be quite warm, the nights are usually cool enough to sleep well, those pesky bugs show up to aggravate you, but one good thing about the summer is that you can get in the water just to cool off and bathe. Now comes autumn and the fall season, the leaves will turn all kind of beautiful colors, the wildlife will be busy gathering food for the winter, and you will prepare for the long winter, also, by getting your food supply built up, feed for your animals, wood stored up to heat and cook with and make any repairs to your shelter that is needed."

That was the most talking Sloppy had done in a week.

Alan smiled as he laid by the warmth of the fire thinking of all that Sloppy had said and nodded off to sleep. Alan was up before daylight stoking the fire and putting coffee on while Yano got up and took the horses and mule to the creek to drink water. Sloppy was awake now, so Alan helped him sit up against a log and handed him a cup of coffee and flatbread with ham to eat. Then it was time to break camp, load their supplies and continue the trip toward home.

On their way again, Alan asked Yano if he could find his way home once they got to Three Bears Trail and he assured his father he could. Alan said, "When we get to Three Bears Trail, I want you to ride on ahead, tell your mother we are bringing Sloppy home, he is very sick and has a broken leg. Tell her to get the shanty by the barn ready for him and put Sloppy's horse, Topper, in the pasture. Then I want you to ride into town and get Dr. Hogue, tell him Sloppy has pneumonia and a broken leg and will be at our house by the time he gets there. Alan told Yano this was another part of the journey to manhood; "I am so proud of you and happy you went with me to help Sloppy."

After about an hour they reached Three Bears Trail and Yano left riding at a fast pace, he should reach home within the hour.

Chapter 6

Yano was met by his very worried mother when he rode up to their home alone without his father. "Where is your father?" Odina asked.

"Yano said, "he is coming, he has Sloppy on a drag sled. He said to tell you Sloppy is very sick with pneumonia and he has a broken leg, Father said to tell you we will put him in the shanty by the barn and for me to ride into town and get Dr. Hogue to come out here to start treating him."

Odina said, "Put Smokie and Topper in the pasture and ride PoGo to town and I will get the shanty ready for Sloppy while you are gone."

Yano put them in the pasture and put a bridle on PoGo and took off to town.

Odina had the other children carried supplies to the shanty while she prepared a pot of potato soup with ham and onions that would help a sick and weak person gain their strength back. She also made some corn fritters. She knew Alan and Yano would need a good meal too.

When Yano got to Dr. Hogue's office, he found another doctor there by the name of Dr. Grant Clark. Dr. Clark said Dr. Hogue had walked across the street to the dining hall, but would be back in a few minutes and asked if he could help him. Yano told him that his father was bringing his sick friend to their house and told him to ride into town to get Dr. Hogue to come to their house.

Dr. Clark asked what his name was, and he said, "I am Yano Adams, my father is Alan Adams, and we live three miles out on Three Bears Trail."

Dr. Clark said he would go get Dr. Hogue and ride with him. "Do you know what is wrong with your father's friend?"

Yano said, he has a broken leg and pneumonia, and my father told me to be sure and tell Dr. Hogue about the pneumonia, so he would know what medicine to bring with him."

"Very well Yano, we will be headed your way shortly."

Yano thanked him and headed home.

It had been a rough two days of riding and Alan was relieved to see his cabin and would be even happier to see his wife and children.

Odina greeted him when they got there and went with him to the shanty to help get Sloppy settled. The children, Ayita, Koda and Nokomis had already stocked the shanty with wood, water, bed linens and candles. Odina told Alan she was cooking a pot of potato soup and making some corn fritters that would be ready in about an hour.

His eyes lit up, he was hungry, and he knew her cooking would also help Sloppy get better.

Shortly, they heard a horse coming up their path and looked to see, it was Yano. Yano said Dr. Hogue and a new doctor, Dr. Clark, were on their way and should be there shortly.

All the Adams stepped out of the shanty, Alan hugged his three youngest children and sent them back to the house. He then hugged Odina and thanked her for all she had done. She smiled; she was so proud of them then she headed back to the house to finish cooking. He asked Yano to stay and sit on the porch of the shanty with him so they could talk. "I'm very proud of you and I couldn't have helped Ole Sloppy without your help. As you grow older you will learn the importance of having friends and helping each other when needed. Always try to have more friends than enemies and always be careful with your words and actions. Honor, respect and doing good deeds build good character and a person with anger and hate builds bad character. You have handled situations better than some grown men I know could have, but you are still a young boy of eleven years old. So, continue being a young boy, honor and respect people, respect mother earth and learn all you can in school then you can be anything you want to be."

They heard a horse and buggy coming up the path and knew it was Dr. Hogue and the new Dr. Clark.

Alan stepped off the porch and motioned for them to come to the shanty. He greeted them both and Dr. Hogue introduced him to Dr. Clark. "He will be my replacement if I ever retire. Now let's check on your friend."

Alan told the doctors his friend's name was Willard Floyd, but everybody called him Sloppy.

Dr Hogue said he knew Sloppy, but didn't see him often, he is a mountain man and doesn't come to town much.

Alan said, "Sloppy has a broken leg and pneumonia, I think, and was just about dead when we found him a week ago. I fed him a little when he would eat, made him some Ginseng tea and did the tapping therapy on his back like I watched you do to Mr. Bolin."

"Let's go in and check him out," said Dr. Hogue.

Alan waited on the porch while both doctors were with him. After about thirty minutes, they came out to talk with him. Dr. Hogue said, "Sloppy is a very sick man, but I have no doubt you saved his life and brought him back from the doorsteps of death." He asked Alan if he had set the bone in his broken leg, it looked good and there was no sign of infection. "No, "Alan said, "Sloppy set his own leg long before I found him."

Dr. Hogue just shook his head, "Ole Sloppy is one tough bird, not many people could do that." Dr. Hogue told Alan that Dr. Grant Clark was a very good doctor and was getting to know the people in this mountain town. He has already helped many of its citizens get well and I am happy to have him. Hearing that from Dr. Hogue was good enough for him to trust Dr. Clark.

Alan invited them to come to the house and have some of Odina's potato soup and corn fritters before leaving for town.

Dr. Hogue knew what a good cook Odina was and accepted the invitation for them both. Dr. Hogue introduced Dr. Clark to Odina and all the children while sitting at the table enjoying supper.

Odina said she was going to take Sloppy a bowl of soup and a corn fritter along with Ginseng tea.

Dr. Hogue said that would do him good if he could eat a little and sip on the hot Ginseng tea.

Alan told Yano to go with his mother and help her while he ate and talked with the doctors.

Dr. Hogue asked Alan where he found Sloppy and how he was able to get him to his place.

Alan said, "Sloppy has a little cabin many miles back in the Appalachian Mountains, it was too far and rough to try and get you there, so I made a drag sled and once he gained some strength, we hauled him out on that sled. It took two days traveling to get back, but I had to get him here to take care of him along with his horse and mule."

"You are a good man Alan, Sloppy is lucky to have a friend like you.

"Thank you, Doc, what are Sloppy's chances of getting better?"

"Well, he's very sick, has double pneumonia and should have already died, but if you can get him to eat and drink plenty of liquids like Ginseng tea, water and even coffee, he should start getting some strength back. You will need to have him sit up in a chair at least two hours every day, one hour each time and do the tapping therapy on his back like you have been doing, twice a day until the pneumonia has cleared up. Because of his age, it may take several months to get his strength back. Dr. Clark or I will come every day and check on him and be sure he puts no weight on that leg until we give the okay to start. The break is as bad as I've ever seen, and it needs to heal before putting any weight on it. In a few days, I would like for him to soak in a hot bath with Epsom salt. If you have a horse trough, that would be perfect, just heat a lot of water and let him soak in it for about thirty minutes."

Odina had returned to the house and told them Sloppy ate half of the potato soup, all the corn fritter and drank a whole cup of Ginseng tea.

That was good news to hear. They stopped by the shanty before heading back to town and told Sloppy to rest all he could, stay off the bad leg until they tell him it's ok to put weight on it and when he is sitting up, to try and cough hard and try to cough up the mucus and flem.

Alan had built an indoor outhouse in the shanty, which was working out well for Sloppy, he wouldn't have to try and go outside.

After Alan had supper, he told Odina all about their trip and what they did to help Sloppy. He said he couldn't have done it without Yano's help. We have some mighty fine children. Odina, I think we are raising them right."

"I agree, said Odina."

Alan said, "I'm going to sit with Sloppy a little while before coming to bed."

Chapter 7

Alan went back to work at the mines in Shepherd Springs, it would be a couple more months before he started traveling to Rockford to oversee the new mine.

Sloppy had gained more of his strength back, but was still too weak to leave, plus he had to use crutches to move around and couldn't put weight on his broken leg yet.

Alan knew Sloppy appreciated what his family was doing for him, but he also knew Sloppy would be happy to be well enough to go back to the life he loved. Alan and the family liked having Sloppy there and were honored to help him get well.

Yano would sit and listen to Sloppy tell stories every chance he got about living in the mountains alone for forty years. Yano has had an adventurous side to him since he was four years old and listening to Sloppy's adventures makes him want to go exploring. He had always paid attention when his father was teaching him life and survival skills and he was learning more from Sloppy's experiences. As soon as he finished his chores, he would head to the shanty and sit with Sloppy for a while to hear more about his adventures. Yano was intrigued by all Sloppy had experienced and really wanted to take off on his own adventure, but he knew his father and mother would not approve. It was alright for him to hunt and fish for food as long as he wasn't gone too long at a time. He asked Sloppy if he would like fish to eat for supper.

"Of course, yes," Sloppy said, "fish would be great."

Yano told his mother he was going to catch some fish for supper and would be back in a little while.

Odina told him it was okay, but she needed more Ginseng roots for tea. "Take your little brother Koda with you and go to the back side of the mountain behind the house for the Ginseng roots before you go to the fishing hole and explain to Koda what the Ginseng plant looks like and which ones to dig up, then y'all can go fishing."

Yano didn't know he was going to have his brother go fishing with him, but he was okay with that. With two shovels and a cloth sack, they start walking to the back side of their property where the Ginseng grows. Yano was always observing his surroundings and when they reached the top of the ridge, he could see rocks on the west side of the mountain. They looked as if they were purposely laid out to form an X mark on the ground. He thought it was odd, but they walked over to the east side of the mountain to dig the Ginseng. He explained to Koda they did not want to deplete the patch of Ginseng; they would only harvest enough from the mature plants to make a few pots of tea. Once they dug up enough roots, they returned to the house and dropped them off to their mother.

Koda was very excited to go fishing with Yano. Yano and Koda doubled up and rode Smokie to the fishing hole. There were already fishing poles stored there, so all they had to do was hunt for bait. Yano knew that finding a rotten log on the ground would almost always have grub worms and bugs hidden underneath it. They found a large log, rolled it over and found six big grub worms. Yano put them in his pocket, they both picked up a fishing pole and slid down the bank to the sandbar where Yano spotted bear tracks. He explained to Koda the bear tracks were old, but bears came through there often, so keep his eyes and ears open while they were fishing.

Koda caught the first fish, it was a sunfish, then he caught another one before Yano had caught anything; Koda laughed and told Yano he was a better fisherman.

Yano smiled at his little brother and told him they needed about eight fish to have enough to feed everybody. Yano told Koda to stay there and fish, he was going downstream a little way to try a couple more deep holes he knew about. They usually held a few fish in the deep holes. About thirty minutes later, Yano returned with four more fish he caught, two trout and two sunfish.

Koda had caught two more sunfish making it four for him as well.

Yano said, "We have enough now, we don't want to catch all the fish here, just enough to eat and feed the family."

When the boys got back home, their father was home from work sitting on the porch of the shanty talking with Sloppy. They cleaned the fish for their mother to cook and Koda started playing in the yard with his sisters while Yano headed down to the shanty to listen to the elders talk. He learned a lot by listening and he wanted to tell them both about how he and Koda went and dug up some Ginseng roots then went to the fishing hole and caught eight fish for supper. As they were walking up in the mountains to dig up the Ginseng roots, Yano said he was observing his surroundings like always and he noticed a rock formation on the ground that was shaped like an X. He thought it was odd those rocks were laying in such a way to form an X on the ground.

His father and Sloppy both looked at Yano as he was talking, with a surprised look on their face. Sloppy knew that was an area marked for some reason and probably marked by his late friend Fred Smith, but he didn't say anything about it. Alan knew the X mark was in the location of the X mark on the other map he found, but he didn't mention anything about it either. He told Yano if he looked at rocks long enough, he could see different shapes and forms just like looking at the clouds, he then changed the subject. Good friends don't even tell good friends everything they know or think they know.

Yano then told them both about the fish he and Koda caught for supper.

Koda came running down to the shanty to tell them to come and eat.

Sloppy used his crutches to get to the house as the rest of them walked along with him.

Alan couldn't understand why he didn't see the rocks formed like an X, but his eleven-year-old son did. He never thought the Ginseng they found in that area was the treasure the X marked, but he would wait before exploring that area. For now, he's more concerned with taking care of Sloppy. When he did explore, he would take Yano with him, so he could explain the importance of being secretive about certain things.

Chapter 8

It was now early September and Sloppy had improved so much, Dr. Hogue had given him the okay to start putting weight on his leg. With Sloppy's improvements coming a couple months quicker than expected, Yano had the hope of going on an adventure alone for a few days. He wanted to go to the northeast end of their property where there was a lake and a small cabin that his father built. He had been there a few times with his father, but really wanted to do this on his own to prove his manhood, if his parents would approve. It was the first of the week and he wanted to go on this adventure early Friday and come back Sunday. When he asked for their permission, he promised to do all his chores before he left and catch them all up when he returned.

Alan and Odina told Yano to let them sleep on it and they would give him an answer tomorrow.

Yano could hardly sleep anticipating what their answer would be. Yano, Koda, Ayita and Nokomis were up early getting chores done before breakfast. Yano was anxious to hear if his parents would let him go on his adventure, but he knew they wouldn't discuss it until after breakfast.

As they all gathered at the table, Alan says grace before they eat.

After breakfast, Alan instructed Yano to hook up PoGo to the buckboard, so he, Ayita and Koda could all ride to school together. He did what his father told him to do, but was hoping he would hear their answer on allowing him to go on his adventure.

Alan walked down to the barn to saddle up Scout and called for Yano to come to him. He said, "Your mother and I have discussed your request and decided to allow you to go on this adventure alone as long as you go to the little cabin and the lake and don't climb on any cliffs. You will need to head back home Sunday, early morning. You can spend two nights at the cabin, and I will allow you to carry my Hawkins Rifle for protection against bears and mountain lions."

Yano was very excited to hear his parents approved, but he knew there would be more orders coming before he left. He must double up on his chores to show his parents they will be done before he leaves. There was a lot of planning to do before Friday such as supplies, he would need to take and what type of exploring he would do.

There was no school on Thursday and Friday which meant he would have more work on Thursday, and he hoped to have time to sit and talk with Sloppy some more. Odina home schooled all her children when they were not in public school. She taught them the Cherokee language and heritage, so they would be able to pass it on to their children.

Wednesday after supper and chores, Yano went and sat on the porch of the shanty to talk with Sloppy. Sloppy knew he was about to go on an adventure alone for a few days, so he felt obligated to tell him a few things. He told Yano the things he needed to know and how to survive in the mountains. "You need food, water and shelter. You can hunt or catch your food. Get your water to drink from a spring, it is the cleanest." Sloppy said, "I know where you are going, so that cabin is your shelter and the tools you need are already there." He said, "you already know a lot, but the most important thing is to know how to recognize the dangers that will be around you."

Sloppy then told Yano that if anything ever happened to him and he should die to remember where he had retrieved the rope and his hat for him at his place and the location of the chair tree. There could be a treasure hidden at the top of that cliff, just look for something out of place, some kind of marking and there may be a treasure at that location. All good prospectors never tell anyone of their secret hiding places so keep this to yourself. He said, "You have been very good to me in my time of need, and I appreciate your friendship. Only after my death, will any of my treasures be yours and that could be twenty or thirty years from now or it could be tomorrow so just remember that spot."

Yano promised to keep the secret and thanked Sloppy for all his lessons about surviving in the mountains. Yano said goodnight to Sloppy and met his father when he was walking back to the house. His father stopped him and told him when he went to the little cabin at the lake to be sure and stay inside when it was dark and when he returned home on Sunday, bring any food from the cabin with him, so the bears won't destroy the cabin trying to get the food.

Alan walked on down and sat with Sloppy for a while on the porch of the shanty. Sloppy told Alan that Yano was very excited to go on his adventure and he seemed very knowledgeable about survivor skills at such a young age. Alan agreed with Sloppy, and he knew Yano just wanted to prove to them that he was approaching manhood, and this was another step in that direction. "I hope his mother and I made the right decision in letting him do that."

It was Thursday morning and Yano was busy cutting firewood, making sure his family had enough to last until he returned. He was thinking of what he would take with him. The little cabin had cooking utensils, an ax, a saw, a hammer, a shovel, extra rope, traps for trapping and pans for panning gold if he wanted to do that. All he would carry with him was the fifty caliber Hawkins Rifle, his bow and arrows, his bed roll and sweet feed and grain for Smokie. He would have to hunt or fish for his food.

Chapter 9

It was breaking daylight when Yano was busy with his chores before breakfast. After breakfast, he would start his adventure, but not before getting more instructions from his father. Alan told him to remember what he had been taught. He said, "respect the land and wildlife, and only take what you need, don't waste anything. Remember the sounds of danger and know that you are alone should you be injured, so don't take any risk. Always take care of your horse, have your firewood supply be enough for warmth and cooking. I don't want you out roaming around after dark, get closed up in the cabin with the Hawkins Rifle until daylight."

After saddling up Smokie and securing his supplies to the saddle, he spoke to Sloppy as he sat on the porch of the shanty drinking coffee.

Sloppy told him that rabbit, squirrel, grouse or fish made a pretty good meal, be safe and we will see you in a few days.

Yano said, "Thanks for everything you taught me Sloppy." Yano rode Smokie up to their front porch to say goodbye to his parents, and brothers and sisters.

Odina handed him a cloth bag with about four biscuits and several slices of bacon, so he wouldn't starve, in case he couldn't trap, hunt or catch his food.

Alan told him to be careful and remember to leave early Sunday morning to come home.

"Yes Sir," Yano said, and started his journey, so excited as he rode out of sight of his family. He felt like it was just him and the mountains now. He rode slowly, observing every tree in the forest, noticing the movement of the squirrels in the trees and the white flags of several startled whitetail deer running away. Yano was in his element, just him and the mountains. After having to go around a few mountains, he arrived at the cabin. He paused long enough to visually inspect the cabin for signs of damage that bears would do, but he didn't see any. He checked the cabin out, removed his supplies from Smokie's back and placed them in the cabin, then began cutting and gathering firewood to heat and cook with. Yano was feeling brave and confident as he hopped on

Smokie to go southwest, following a small stream to do some exploring. He rode Smokie until it got too rough and dangerous, so he tied Smokie to a tree, removed the Hawkins Rifle from the scabbard and walked about another two or three hundred yards further downstream. He had to climb over some large rocks while staying in line with the stream when he noticed a sharp bend in the stream, then he could see a sandbar with very dark sand and a lot of small rocks at the edge of it. He knew that dark sand was supposed to be a good place to pan for gold, but he didn't have a shovel or pan with him. That would be something good for him to do tomorrow when he could be more prepared, so he started walking back upstream to get Smokie and go back to the cabin.

Once back at the cabin, Yano removed the saddle from Smokie and put him in the small coral that was attached to the west side of the cabin. He had already cut enough firewood for the wood stove in the cabin, so he got busy gathering dead limbs to build a fire outside in the fire-pit between the cabin and stream. He thought if he built a big fire outside, it would help keep the bears and mountain lions away. Yano was feeling like a real mountain man and loved being in the mountains alone for the first time. He decided he wanted to have fish for supper, so he went to the lake that was about fifty yards behind the cabin. There were several large boulders along the edge of the lake that made for a good place to sit and think while fishing. Yano climbed up on one of the large rocks with his fishing pole and Hawkins Rifle. With his baited hook in the water, he leaned back against the rock and heard a Red Tail Hawk high in the sky above him. He remembered his father telling him to always listen to the sounds around him and he would learn the language of the wildlife. Yano sat there with his eyes closed, feeling the warmth of the sun shining down on him, listening to the sounds of nature around him when he felt a tug on his fishing pole. He pulled out a trout which was big enough to make a meal for him, so he stopped fishing for now. Yano tied a string to the trout and put it back in the water until he was ready to go. He laid back down again on the big rock with his eyes closed to enjoy the feeling of the sun and sounds around him. He nodded off to sleep laying on the rock until he was awakened by the sound of a deer blowing at him. Four deer were passing behind him and were startled when they got his scent. Yano was startled too when he heard the deer blowing at him. He jumped up to see the deer running off. He knew what deer sounded like when they were frightened or curious about something, but when he was awakened by that loud sound right behind him, it scared him a little at first. Enough resting on the rock, he walked back to the cabin to check on Smokie and clean the fish that he would cook for supper later.

Once his chores were done, he was off exploring again to the east of the cabin. Yano spotted all kinds of wildlife tracks and could tell that a rabbit trail was going in a brush pile, so he set a snare on the rabbit trail hoping to catch a rabbit to eat tomorrow. He walked until he came to some very steep rock cliffs that he really wanted to climb and explore, but he didn't because of his father's orders not too and remembering his father telling him if he got injured, he would be alone, so he didn't want that. Yano did climb about halfway up a hill to just sit and observe things. He had the fifty caliber Hawkins Rifle with him for protection, but had no intention of using it for small game, he would use his bow and arrow for small game, the Hawkins was to be used against bears and mountain lions if needed.

The sun was going down, so he started walking back to the cabin. He was getting hungry, but first he had to take care of Smokie before cooking up the trout he caught. Yano fed Smokie and made sure he had plenty of water then went inside the cabin and built a fire in the wood stove to warm it up and cook his supper. He had a fire laid outside in the firepit, but he would not light it until he cooked and ate his supper.

After eating the trout and a biscuit his mother had sent with him, he went outside and lit a fire in the firepit. It was pitch-black dark now so after the fire got going good Yano went back in and closed himself up in the cabin just as his father had ordered him to do. Just as he was securing the door, he heard the loudest eerie scream that sounded like a baby screaming right on the front porch. He was pretty sure it wasn't on the porch, but he knew the sound was a Bobcat not a mountain lion. Smokie was nervous and neighing out in the coral. Yano grabbed the Hawkins Rifle and went out in the dark to check on Smokie. When Smokie calmed down, Yano returned to the cabin and secured himself inside. This would be his first night alone staying in the cabin deep in the mountains and he would do as his father told him to do and stay in the cabin while it was dark. The loud scream of the Bobcat scared him enough that he had no problem staying in the cabin. He remembered his father telling him that a Bobcat sounded like a baby screaming and a mountain lion sounded like a woman screaming. He didn't fear the Bobcat, but the screaming sound they make would frighten anyone for a second.

Yano laid down on his bunk, thinking of what he wanted to explore tomorrow. The first thing would be to check the snare he set for a rabbit. If no rabbit was in the snare, he would remove it and hunt for a squirrel or grouse for his supper with his bow and arrow. He wanted to pan for gold at the place he found with the black sand. He heard the hooting of an Owl, off in the distance, as he nodded off to sleep.

After a few hours of restful sleep, he awakened to the sound of birds chirping and light coming through the window of the cabin. He could see his breath because of the chill inside the cabin, so he built a fire in the wood stove and put on a pot of water to make sassafras tea to have with his bacon and biscuit. Yano got dressed and stepped out onto the porch and surveyed his surroundings for anything of danger. The fire in the firepit was out and appeared to have kept bears and mountain lions away during the night. When checking on Smokie, he looked at the lake behind the cabin to see a misty fog laying on top of the water. He picked up his Hawkins Rifle, that he shoots well with accuracy, even though it was as long as he was tall and headed out to check the snare. He had caught a rabbit in the snare and knew it would be enough for his supper tonight. After he had breakfast, he cleaned the rabbit and wrapped it in a cool damp cloth until it was time to prepare it later.

Yano gathered more wood to use tonight for the firepit, then saddled up Smokie to begin his adventure of the day. His plan was to go back to where he saw the black sand on the edge of the stream west of the cabin and pan for gold. He loaded up the short handle shovel, the pan for panning gold and the Hawkins Rifle and started his adventure. He traveled slowly following the stream and observing the landscape as he went. He was intrigued by all the different trees and large rocks that were all along the mountain side. Yano had been riding for about thirty minutes; there was a light breeze blowing through the mountain hollows, enough that he could see the trees swaying slightly. As he topped a small hill, something told him to stop and look around that area. When he looked to his left, where the stream was down below him, he spotted four deer standing on the other side, frozen in their stance, looking at him. Yano was sitting on Smokie staying perfectly still and couldn't believe what he was seeing. It had been seven years since he had seen the ghost deer, but there it was, not twenty or thirty yards from him. He knew it was not the same deer he saw when he was four because this one had a patch of brown on his shoulder and another patch of brown on his hind quarter. He knows it was the Piebald that carried the spirit of change and per his elders, he was prohibited from killing the Piebald deer. Yano was feeling honored to have seen two Piebald deer in his young years. He and the deer were staring at each other for what seemed like five minutes when he heard that familiar alert sound. The Piebald deer blew the alarm and all four took off with their white (flags) tails raised. Yano sat there a few more minutes before he continued his journey. The Piebald deer was a buck with what looked like a six- or eight-point rack. Today was the last day of his adventurous trip, but he already had so much to tell his parents about his experience, and he had many hours left to explore more.

Traveling a few more minutes, he arrived at the spot where he had to stop and go the rest of the way on foot. Before he dismounted, he sat and checked the terrain out for any sign of danger. The light breeze had completely stopped, and the forest was perfectly still. As he hopped off Smokie and was untying the shovel from the back of the saddle, he heard the very distinctive sound of a howling Wolf. Yano had goosebumps on his arms and was frightened of the sound at first, but then he remembered his father telling him to respect the Spirit of the Wolf and the location of the howling Wolf might be where treasures could be found. This memory excited him because the location of the howling Wolf was where he was headed to pan for gold. Nervously standing there beside Smokie, he wasn't sure he really wanted to go to that location, but his curiosity to explore got the best of him, so he removed the Hawkins Rifle from the scabbard, put the shovel, some rope and the gold pan in a burlap bag, so he could carry them easier and with caution, started walking to the location. Every few steps, he would stop, look and listen before walking a few more steps. When he arrived at the location, he paused and looked the terrain over real good again for any signs of danger. Since he saw no threats or heard no sounds of danger, he started digging with the shovel. At first, he dug up shovels full of small pebbles and after inspecting each small rock, he dug down under the pebbles to try and get more sand. Yano started picking out the small rocks and throwing them off to the side, then he took the pan, dipped it into the water, so he could swish it around to sling out the bad sand. He found two gold nuggets about the size of a small acorn that came from a water oak tree. Yano was so excited now that he forgot to scan his surroundings for danger. He put the two nuggets in his shirt pocket and got another shovel full from the same place and found three more gold nuggets in that shovel full.

Yano sat back on the sandbar, and started thinking about what he had been taught by his elders and the experiences he had in the last two days of his adventure. Seeing the Piebald deer and being told that it meant change was coming, then the howling of the Wolf. He remembered his father and their friend Sloppy saying a prospector keeps it a secret of what he found and where he found the treasures.

Yano now has five gold nuggets in his shirt pocket and decided to stop digging for gold now. He marked the spot by placing two logs in an X shape just above the stream then went back to check on Smokie. He really didn't want to leave this place, but now he knew what was there and it would be a place he could come back to with more tools to work with. He had more exploring to do before it got too late, when it got dark, he would close himself up in the cabin until daylight then he would head home like his father told him. He rode Smokie southwest to see land he hadn't seen before. Some of the mountains were steep with large boulders everywhere he looked. After riding about half a mile, he spotted a tree shaped like a chair at the base of one of the mountains. Yano remembered the chair tree that was at Sloppy's place and Sloppy telling him that the Indians would bend and shape a sapling to grow in different shapes so they could use them as a marker for directional purpose or a place of importance. When he surveyed the mountain side, he could see what he believed to be a cave about fifty feet high up on a steep mountain side with large boulders. He knew it was too dangerous for him to explore alone, but he would remember its location because of the chair tree.

The cave really had his interest so much that he just sat and stared at it. As he kept his eyes focused on the darkness of the cave, he noticed the movement of what appeared to be three or four little figures moving around at the mouth of the cave. His first thought was they were bear cubs, but being so small and far away he wondered if they could be Wolf pups. Wolves had been eradicated from the area for fifty years. Yano could not see if the little critters had tails or not, which would have helped identify them, if only he could see them better. He was more excited now about this find, but also glad he didn't climb up there to explore because the mother of the newborns would be very protective of her young.

Leaving the area, he continued southwest a little further before going back to the cabin. He was seeing so much of the land and had traveled a long way from the cabin and the trail that led to the cabin. When he stopped at the bottom of the mountain range to look around, he spotted a bear on the side of the mountain to his right about one hundred yards from him. The bear was just above a laurel thicket, it appeared to be feeding on huckleberries. His first thought was this could be the mama bear to the little critters he saw at the cave, but that would remain a mystery until he asked his father to come with him to verify what they were. Quietly, he left the area, and headed back to the cabin, it was getting to be late afternoon and he had things to do before dark.

When he got to the cabin, he removed the saddle from Smokie and put him in the coral with feed and water. Next, he built a fire in the cook stove so he could cook the rabbit for supper and after eating, he built a fire outside in the fire-pit. He then closed himself up in the cabin until daylight. Yano was all smiles laying on his bunk with a full belly thinking of everything he had seen and done. Laying there, he heard the hoot of an Owl again off in the distance.

Yano knew he would be too excited to not tell his father about finding the gold, but his father would be the only one he told, unless his father approved of him telling the rest of the family. He would also tell him about finding the chair tree with what appeared to be a cave on the mountain side above it. He had so much to tell about his adventure, what wildlife he saw, the animal sounds he heard, the food he caught and the landscape he was able to explore. He was tired enough; he fell asleep pretty quick.

Chapter 10

With daylight peeking through the window and the sound of birds chirping, it was time for Yano to get up and get ready to head home like his father told him. First, he built a small fire in the wood stove, so he could heat up the pot of remaining sassafras tea and have the last biscuit with bacon. With a little food in his belly, he started gathering everything he needed to carry back home. He had saddled Smokie, put the Hawkins in the scabbard, tied his bedroll on the back along with all the remaining food in the saddle bags. He made sure the fire was out in the wood stove, secured the cabin and left.

Yano made it home around ten in the morning. He stopped at the front porch and watched his brother and sisters playing outside before taking the rifle and remaining food inside. His mother was in the kitchen and so happy her first born was home. She made sure he knew how proud she was of him. His mother said, "You know your father is very proud also and is waiting to see you, he is over at the shanty talking with Sloppy."

Yano left the house to take Smokie to the barn and release him into the pasture before walking over to the shanty where his father and Sloppy were sitting on the porch both anxiously waiting to hear about his adventure.

Alan was so relieved and proud to see his son back at home smiling and uninjured.

Yano was excited to begin telling his father and Sloppy about his adventures beginning with gathering firewood, making sure he had enough for heat as well as the fire pit and cooking. He told of catching a large trout big enough for supper his first night, the deer blowing at him as he nodded off to sleep on a big rock at the lake. Awakened by the deer, he got moving again exploring the west side, then returned to the cabin, put Smokie in the coral, and decided to explore the east side. He found many tracks and set a snare hoping to catch a rabbit for supper the next night. Back again at the cabin, it was time to feed and water Smokie and close up the cabin, but just as he secured the door, a Bobcat let out the most eerie scream making Smokie nervous, so he grabbed the rifle and went out to check and calm Smokie down. Finally, it was time to get some sleep with only a hoot owl in the distance.

The next morning after breakfast, it was time to check on the snare, in luck, he had caught a rabbit for supper. He began to dress the rabbit by cleaning and wrapping it in a cool damp cloth so it would be ready to cook later. After gathering up more wood for the fire-pit, it was time to saddle up Smokie and ride southwest to explore further than the day before. He saw another ghost deer that was with three brown deer. When the deer spooked and ran off, he continued to explore finding another chair tree at the bottom of the mountain. As he looked up toward the steep mountain far above the large rock ledges, he spotted a cave. Trying to keep his focus on the cave, he noticed some movement. There appeared to be three or maybe four little figures, the best he could tell. They were too far off to tell, at first, he thought they could be bear cubs, but what if they were wolf pups? The mountain was too steep to climb by himself to get a closer look, but he remembered it was near the chair tree and he was thinking they could go back later and check it out together. He left there and went further south and spotted a bear on the mountain side feeding on huckleberries so he was thought maybe the bear could be the mama to the little critter he saw at the mouth of the cave. Yano thought for a minute and decided not to say anything about finding the gold or hearing the howl of the Wolf until he could talk to his father alone.

Sloppy said, "Were you ever scared while you were alone?"

Yano said, "Yes; once when the Bobcat screamed and, also, I was startled when the deer blew behind me while I was sleeping on the rock. I recovered quickly once I knew what made the sounds." Alan and Sloppy beamed with pride to see the honesty in Yano, they knew anybody would be startled at first when hearing the sounds if they were truthful.

Alan was interested in hearing about the rest of his son's experiences, but he explained to Yano they would have to wait a little later, since he had chores that needed to be done.

Yano totally understood and left to do the chores like he promised he would when he returned from his adventure.

As Yano started his chores, Alan and Sloppy continued talking on the porch. Sloppy told Alan he felt well enough now to go back to his home in the mountains. He said, "Thanks to you and Odina, I have my strength back and can walk now. My horse and mule are healthy again and I've intruded on your kindness long enough."

Alan was sad that Sloppy wanted to leave, but he knew this time would come and he completely understood how much he loved the mountain life that he had lived for the past forty years.

Sloppy asked if they would let him have some coffee, cornmill and feed for his horse and mule, he would repay them in a couple of weeks when he went to town to trade or sell things to Beanstalk.

Alan said, "sure, we can give you what supplies you need." He had really enjoyed having Sloppy staying with them and was glad he was well enough to go home, but he sure would miss his friend.

Sloppy said, "I will leave in the morning and I'm so thankful for your friendship, your caring kindness, and the medical treatments that healed me. I will do my best to repay y'all for all you have done for me."

Alan said, "You don't owe us anything, just promise you will come back and know you are family to us and always welcome."

Sloppy joined the Adams' family at the supper table and told Odina and the children he was leaving in the morning. They were all sad; to them Sloppy was one of the family and they were hoping he would live with them forever.

Yano was really sad; he had learned so much from Sloppy and would miss his talks.

Sloppy told them all he would return often and stay a few days each time, if that was okay, which made them all feel a little better, knowing he would return from time to time.

After supper, Alan told Yano when he went to the barn to take care of the livestock to put about twenty pounds of sweet feed, grain and oats in burlap bags for Sloppy to take with him.

Odina said she would bag up some food supplies and coffee for him to take.

Koda went with Yano to help while the girls helped their mother in the kitchen.

Alan and Sloppy took a cup of coffee with them to the porch and Alan told him there would always be a place for him if he needed it or wanted it. Sloppy was sad to leave, but excited to get back to his place and live off the land for as long as he was able.

When morning came, the children were up doing their chores as Odina started preparing breakfast and Alan was helping Sloppy gather his things to take back to his home in the mountains. After breakfast, Alan would go to work at the Shepherd Springs Coal Mines, and the children would take the buckboard to school and Sloppy would pack up and go home.

Yano had not yet told his father about finding gold and hearing the howling of the Wolf, but he planned on telling him later in the evening, when he got home. As Yano was hooking up PoGo to the buckboard, he spoke with Sloppy and helped him load his supplies on the mule. He used this time to say his goodbyes and to thank him for his stories and lessons about mountain living.

Sloppy thanked Yano too for all he had done for him and told him not to forget what he told him about the chair tree at the location where he retrieved his rope and hat. "It's very important that you remember that area."

Yano asked, "What will I find there Sloppy?"

Sloppy just smiled at him and said, "Not now, only after I pass away, are you to look and then look for something that might look a little out of place for the area."

Ayita and Koda came down and hopped on the buckboard to ride to school with Yano. Alan had already left for work. Odina had bagged up plenty of food supplies along with coffee for Sloppy to take home and said her goodbyes, as she sadly watched him ride off.

There was a sad quietness at the Adams' homestead now. Odina would clean up the kitchen, then start making her Indian jewelry that Beanstalk had requested. She would, also, homeschool their youngest daughter, Nokomis, for a couple of hours during the day.

The children got home from school around two thirty and Odina instructed the boys to bring in more firewood for the fireplace and wood stove after they put PoGo in the pasture. After those chores were finished, she told Yano to kill one of the red chickens that had stopped laying, and they would have fried chicken tonight.

Alan rode up around four thirty and went straight to the barn to put Scout up before walking up to the house.

Yano told Koda to take the chicken to their mother, he was going to help his father down at the barn. Yano told his father he didn't tell him everything about his trip because of what he was taught by him. He said, "You taught me to be secretive on certain things, but I wanted to tell you about finding gold and I'm sure there is more where I found it. When I was out exploring the first day, I rode Smokie as far as I could go southwest and followed the little stream that runs in front of the cabin. Then, I walked a few hundred yards further downstream and spotted a sandbar with black sand and I remembered hearing you say that's usually a good place to search for gold."

Alan just stood listening to his son and feeling very proud of him.

Yano said, "I had no tools or gold pan to work with, so I decided to come back the next day with the tools I needed. The next morning, I carried the shovel and gold pan and again I rode Smokie as far as I could, that's when I saw the ghost deer. When the deer ran off, I tied Smokie to a tree and was removing the shovel when I heard the howling of the Wolf that sounded like it was exactly where I had found the black sand. I just stood there a few minutes debating on going to that place or not, I decided to go. I carried the rifle, shovel and gold pan and slowly, walked to the location, looking for any sign of the Wolf and listening for any danger sounds. When I got there, I scanned the area really good, then started digging up one shovel full of small rocks and a little black sand. I dumped that shovel full into the pan and started picking out the rocks to throw them out of the way, then, dipping the pan in the creek, so I could swish out the bad sand. I never noticed any flakes of gold, but there were two nuggets the size of water oak acorns in the first shovel full. I then got my second shovel full and found three nuggets about the same size. I stopped after finding a total of five good size nuggets and marked the area by placing logs on the side of the bank to form an X. I knew

I needed to tell you about this find, but not to say anything to anyone else."

Alan said, "I'm proud of you Yano, for the way you handled yourself on your adventure. Those five nuggets will be yours. I want you to show me on the plat, where this location is on that section of land, but know that we are family and treasures found on family land belong to family for everyone's future."

Yano said he understood and wanted to go back with Koda and more tools to see what they could find.

Alan said, "That might be allowed later, but there is no hurry because you know where it is and that's just like money in the bank. I want you to concentrate on your schoolwork and chores here at home for now."

Yano didn't like that answer too much, but he would do as his father said.

Alan told him he wanted to tell his mother about what he had found, and Yano agreed, feeling she would also be proud of him.

Chapter 11

After supper, Alan got the plat out and laid it on the table while Yano retrieved his five nuggets to show his mother and father. With the plat on the table, Alan showed Yano where the cabin was and pointed to the stream.

Yano took his finger, and followed the stream until it made a sharp left turn and said, "That is the spot." Yano told them both again how the Bobcat screaming that first night scared him for a few seconds, but then he was alright because he knew it wasn't a mountain lion.

Alan didn't tell Odina that when he said he and Sloppy were going into town to visit Roosters Tavern for a while and wouldn't be back until after dark, he really went to the far end of their land to check on Yano. Alan told her he spoke a half-truth, Sloppy really did go to Roosters Tavern. When they went to bed, he told her the truth, he just wanted to make sure his son was safe. He tied Scout to a tree and walked a few hundred yards more to the cabin and hid behind a large tree where he watched Yano build the fire in the fire pit then go inside the cabin.

That's when he made the sound of a Bobcat to see Yano's reaction. His fake Bobcat scream upset Smokie, and he saw Yano come out of the cabin with the rifle in hand to protect Smokie. After he calmed Smokie down he went back in and closed himself up in the cabin.

Odina laughed a little, leaned over and kissed her husband saying, "You are a good father, Alan Adams, and I already knew you didn't go to Roosters Tavern, it's hard to fool an Indian, but wait until Yano is much older before you tell him that you were the Bobcat that scared him, we don't want him to know right now that we were worried. We'll just let him know how proud we are of him."

Alan smiled and said, "Yes Dear." before they fell asleep.

The morning came and you could hear the rooster crowing.

Odina and Alan were already up, coffee was made. Alan built a fire in the fireplace to warm the house while Odina started working on breakfast for their family of six. All the children are slowly getting up and doing their chores before breakfast. After breakfast, three of the children would take the buckboard to school.

Alan and Yano went to the barn, Alan saddled up Scout and Yano hooked up PoGo to the buckboard. While at the barn, he reminded Yano to not mention anything to anybody about what he found, if the wrong people heard about it, they could cause harm to our family.

Yano said he understood and would keep it a secret.

This was the first morning in a long time that their friend Sloppy was not at the breakfast table and everyone was missing him, but they knew he was happy to get back to his mountain life.

It was lunchtime and Alan rode into town and met with Mr. Stockburn at the Tibbs Dining Hall for lunch. Mr. Stockburn advised Alan; he would need to catch the train to Rockford on Monday morning to help get things set up for the opening of the mining operation. He said there would be a room at the hotel reserved for him and John Thomas. They could have their meals there, also, and the company would pay for them weekly. There was a livery stable close by where they could rent a horse and saddle, or he could take his own horse by train.

Alan said he understood and thanked Mr. Stockburn for the opportunity and he would probably purchase another horse there and either board it or ride it back and forth every three or four days. The hardest part would be being away from his family for three days every week, but he was very thankful to Mr. Stockburn for working with him and making it possible for him to accept the position, he wasn't willing to move his family to Rockford, Virginia.

When the children got home from school, and Alan got home from work, after supper, Alan let them know the new job started next Monday and he would be gone three days at a time, but nothing would change for them at home. They were still required to do their chores every day, go to school every day and not wander off to far from the house, and he looked directly at Yano when he said it, no long distance exploring and mind your mother.

Odina looked at Alan and smiled, she knew that he knew she could take care of business, but it was nice to hear him say that. For the next few days, Alan and his sons were busy gathering firewood so they would have enough for cooking and staying warm. Alan told Yano not to go to the lake cabin while he was out of town. The weekend he returned from Rockford, he would go with him, and he could show him the cave where he saw the small critters and the place where he found his treasures. When Yano was telling him about seeing the little critters at the cave, but couldn't tell what they were because of the distance, he had this feeling of the possibility they might be Wolf pups. Yano said he saw three or four, it's rare that a black bear has four cubs, but not Wolves. Alan would check with Beanstalk at the Trading Post about purchasing a telescope to use to see if he could identify the critters from a distance.

It was now Wednesday and Alan has completed his first three days of work in Rockford, arriving home late Wednesday night. He wasn't fond of riding the train, but it was quicker than horseback. Rockford Virginia was about sixty miles northeast of Shepherd Springs and it took about two and half hours each way by train. Alan was excited to see his wife and children as they were to see him. Yano was especially excited, since his father said they would go to the cabin at the lake the weekend after he returned from Rockford to check out the little critters at the cave and the spot where he found the gold nuggets.

Odina fixed Alan a bowl of her delicious potato soup; she and the children had already eaten a couple hours earlier. They all gathered around the table with Alan asking the children how their three days were with their chores and schooling.

Their youngest daughter, Nokomis, spoke to her father in Cherokee.

Alan smiled and told her how proud he was of her for learning the language of their ancestors.

Odina said, "They were all well behaved, did their chores and were doing well with their education, Yano never wandered off too far from the house even though she thought he really wanted to."

Sending all the children to bed, Alan got another cup of coffee and sat in front of the fireplace telling Odina about his first three days. He had a room and ate his meals at the hotel that the Coal Mining Company paid for. He rented a horse from the livery stable to ride to the mines. Jacob Bolin and his wife had been there for a couple of months now, and he was doing a good job as the Safety Officer and Supervisor. He told Odina he would go to the Shepherd Springs Coal Mine in the morning and Friday because John Thomas had gone to Rockford. They would share the responsibilities of both mines. After lunch Friday, he and Yano would go to the cabin at the lake and spend just one night there, he really wanted to see if he could see if he could see the little critters that Yano saw. He had the feeling they might be Wolf pups and if they were, it would mean they were making a comeback from extinction. Alan was more interested in finding out about the little critters than he was about the gold location Yano found.

Alan, Odina, Yano and their good friend Sloppy had all heard the howling of the Wolf, but never found any sign that they existed. Alan was the only one that had seen the ghost like image of a Wolf, but still never found any tracks. He couldn't explain why nobody had seen tracks or kill sights of the Wolf, but the Spirit of the Wolf lived on in the Appalachian Mountains.

Chapter 12

It was now Friday morning and Yano had no school today, so Alan told him to finish his chores and then get the supplies they would need together and when he got home around lunch, they would ride out to the cabin at the lake. He told him to be sure to load up some food because they wouldn't have time to hunt or fish for their food. Alan traded some of Odina's Indian jewelry to Beanstalk for a telescope. The telescope would help him identify the little critters especially if he could see them.

Both father and son were excited as they rode to the cabin. When they reached the cabin, they unloaded their supplies and Alan told Yano to lead them to the cave if he could find it. Yano said he could find it because it was where he found the chair tree and should only take ten or fifteen minutes to get there. Yano led the way as his father watched his son. In fifteen minutes, they arrived at the chair tree, and both quietly dismounted. Yano pointed to the cave that was about forty or fifty feet up on the side of the mountain. As they both stared at the opening of the cave, they saw no movement, so Alan decided to climb a tree that was in line with the cave for a better look. He managed to climb up about thirty feet and propped himself on a limb. Looking through the telescope, it was so dark in the cave he could not see the back of the cave, still not seeing any movement, he waited. Then he thought he saw something moving forward toward the mouth of the cave. With his telescope focused on the movement, he could now see it. Looking at the little critter, he could see its ears, its snout and its tail and knew it was not bear cubs. Then three more little critters came out from the back of the cave. Alan looked down to the ground and could see Yano smiling, he could see them too. He continued to study the critters using the telescope. He was certain they were not Fox kits. The Red Wolf had been completely eradicated from that region for over fifty years, but he was looking at four Wolf pups that Yano found two weeks ago. Alan watched the four pups play with each other at the opening of the cave, but didn't see any more movement deeper in the cave. There was a thin ledge that ran to the left of the cave entrance, and he could see, using his telescope, how the ledge allowed the Wolf to get to the cave. The pups were running and playing back and forth on the ledge. He remained perched on the limb hoping to see the mother to the pups, but she never showed up. When he started to climb down from the tree, the pups noticed his movement and ran back to the cave. Alan asked Yano if he knew what it meant to have four wolf pups in that cave.

Yano gave him a puzzled look and said, "It means they have a mother somewhere."

Alan said, "Yes and a father too." To Alan this was better than finding gold. He said, "Yano, let's sneak out of here, so we don't disturb them. You have found an amazing treasure in finding the wolf pups, and I am proud of you for not climbing up that steep mountain to get a better look when you were here by yourself."

Yano asked his father if he wanted him to show him the place where he found the other treasures.

Alan said, "Yes, let's go grab the shovel and pan first, then we will see what we can find." When they got to Yano's secret spot and dug their first shovel full of small rocks and sand and they found two nuggets that were a little bigger than the ones Yano had found earlier. Another shovel full had several flakes of gold, but no nuggets. They panned several more pans of sand and found a lot more flakes. Digging deeper, they came up with more of the small rocks that had three more nuggets, a little smaller than the first two.

Alan said they would stop for now and fix the place back like it was, so it wouldn't look like they had been digging there. "You know exactly where it is, but keep quiet or there could be thieves who would sneak in here and steal your gold."

Yano said he understood, and he was happy his father came with him.

Returning to the cabin, they put their horses in the coral and fed and watered them. Odina had sent plenty of food for them. Inside the cloth bag was corn fritters, biscuits, a slab of bacon, a large jar of her delicious potato soup, six eggs and coffee. Alan wanted to use this time to talk to Yano about making the cabin a little bigger, so the whole family could make trips up there and enjoy the lake and land. He told Yano he wanted him to start drawing up plans for the cabin addition. Think of what it would take to make it big enough for six people to have a place to sleep and a large counter space for prepping food. Then you would need to figure out how much lumber as well as what size lumber it would take. This would require you to use your brain to get the measurements and the supplies needed. "When I am at work in Rockford for three days, I don't want you coming up here until I get home. When you do come back, I want you to start bringing Koda with you, so you can teach him how to pan for gold and how important it is to keep it a secret. This is our family's land and everything on it belongs to our family. We want you and your brother and sisters to continue your education, learn to do many things and never rely on prospecting for gold as a living. Prospecting for gold and gemstones would be a good hobby and could be financial security, if you found a lot of it, but if you don't manage your treasures, you would need to know other ways to survive. You can always set aside time for prospecting, but don't get so tied up in it that you forget your other duties and chores.

After supper, they sat around the firepit outside with the temperature probably in the thirties making the fire feel good. Alan said when they left in the morning he wanted to go back to where the cave was, get on top of the ridge above it and see what he could see. He said there had to be some wolf sign somewhere since they got into the cave. "We may try to come back in a couple of weeks to check on the Wolf pups, this is a very important find you have found Yano. The Spirit of the Wolf lives in these Appalachian Mountains." As they turned in for the night, Yano laid his bedroll out on the floor while his father took the only bunk in the cabin. When morning came, Yano was up getting the fire going in the wood stove. It was cold in the cabin, but warmed up pretty quick. Alan put on a pot of coffee, then started cooking breakfast from the supply Odina sent. After breakfast, they saddled up the horses and started their ride to the mountain where the cave was again. Once there, Alan knew he probably wouldn't be able to see the cave from the top, so he told Yano to go to the chair tree and let him know when he was directly over the cave when he went up the ridge. He could see Yano standing at the chair tree at the bottom, when Yano gave the sign that he was lined up with the cave, Alan marked the spot by stacking a few rocks so he would know the cave was directly under the stacked rocks. He then took his telescope, looking over the edge of the rock face cliff, and tried to spot wolf tracks or any kind of sign as to how they traveled to the cave. He could not see any sign on the ledge or find any sign of a trail the wolves would have used to get there. It was hard for him to understand why he couldn't see any sign from the wolves, especially since he and Yano had seen the four Wolf pups. Alan eased himself off the top of the mountain and met back up with Yano at the chair tree at the bottom.

Now, they were ready to head back home, but Alan didn't want to use the good trail he made getting to the cabin, he wanted to go further west to look for wolf signs. He knew if they continued southwest, they would come out on Three Bears Trail. Alan and Yano talked as they were riding and looking for wolf tracks, he told Yano not to tell any of his friends about seeing the Wolf pups or finding gold, but he would like to tell Sloppy about the Wolf pups. He knew he would be excited to learn they were making a comeback in this area, and they wouldn't have to worry about him trying to trap them on their land.

Yano understood the reason more now for certain secrets he kept. They were seeing bear tracks, deer tracks, mountain lion tracks, fox tracks, opossum tracks, bobcat tracks and rabbit tracks, but no wolf tracks. He just couldn't understand how they couldn't be any wolf tracks when he saw the Wolf pups, knowing there was at least one adult male and one adult female wolf in the area.

Chapter 13

They make it to Three Bears Trail and headed south toward home. As they were riding along, Alan could see two sets of tracks, one from a horse and the other from a mule and he knew exactly who it was. He smiled and told Yano Ole Sloppy was ahead of them, "let's see if we can catch up with him?" They picked up the pace a little and within a few minutes, they could see a man with a floppy hat on a horse pulling a mule behind him.

Yano took off and caught up with him, he was excited to see his friend and so was Alan. Now all three were riding together at a walking pace. Sloppy said he was going into town to get supplies, but would like to stay a couple of nights in the shanty, if that would be okay. Alan was pleased to hear that, and Sloppy knew he was always welcome to stay with them as long as he wanted to. He came so close to losing his first friend and having him stay with them made him feel better and gave them both time to talk. Yano liked sitting and talking with Sloppy too. Alan told Yano to ride on ahead and tell his mother Sloppy was coming to stay a few days.

"Yes Sir, says Yano and he took off to tell his mother."

When Alan and Sloppy arrived at the house, Odina and Nokomis had already carried bedding and coffee down to the shanty, while the twins, Koda and Ayita were stocking it up with firewood. They were all happy to see Sloppy and glad that he would be staying with them a few days or as long as he wanted.

Sloppy smiled, said his hellos and told them all how glad he was to see them.

Odina said, "I hope you have a big appetite Sloppy; we are preparing a fine supper tonight."

Sloppy just smiled and says, "I've never known you to cook a bad meal, Odina."

Alan helped Sloppy put his things in the shanty and then it was time for porch sitting and talking. Meanwhile, Yano took all the horses and the mule to the barn and released them into the pasture.

Alan looked Sloppy in the eye and asked how it had been going for him for the last few weeks being back at his place.

Sloppy said, "It's been hard, I don't have the wind in me that I once had and my leg aches pretty bad when I do too much walking. Now don't get me wrong, I still love the mountain life, I feel at peace when I'm there, it's just that I can't do now what I could do a year ago. I have been able to catch fish to eat and snare some rabbits too, but I no longer can handle a long trap line. I can still do a little prospecting and that helps to pay for my supplies."

It would be a few more hours before they would have supper, so Alan and Sloppy were enjoying the pot of coffee they made and while they sat on the porch and talked. They saw Yano walking to the shanty and Alan knew he wanted to tell Sloppy about the Wolf pups he found. Alan had already told Yano it would be okay to tell Sloppy about the Wolf pups, he would keep it a secret. Yano told them he had all the horses and mule taken care of so Alan says, why don't you tell Sloppy what kind of critters you found.

Yano got this big smile on his face and told Sloppy he found Wolf pups, four of them, they thought.

Sloppy gave him a puzzled look and says, "Wow, that's exciting news and then looked at Alan as if to ask if that was true."

Alan nodded his head yes; he saw them too. He told Sloppy that Yano spotted three or four little critters at the mouth of a cave up high on a mountain side two weeks ago when he was on his adventure. At first, Yano thought they were bear cubs, but wasn't sure since he couldn't get close enough to tell. Alan said, "I went back there with him a couple of weeks later with a telescope hoping to get a look at what he found. The cave that he located was about forty or fifty feet up on the steep side of the mountain, so I climbed up a tree about twenty-five or thirty feet high, got in line with the cave and watched until I saw movement. I knew right away they were not bear cubs or fox kits. When I finally got a good look at the four little critters, I knew without a doubt they were Wolf pups."

Sloppy spoke up and said, "this means the Red Wolf that has been gone, eradicated entirely from this region of the Appalachians for over fifty years, is making a comeback and that is very exciting, but everybody don't need to know it."

Alan said, "that's what I told Yano, we don't want a lot of people coming here to hunt or trap them." He also told Sloppy that seeing the pups meant there was a male and female adult in the area, but no sign could be found. We've not found any kill sights, trails, or wolf tracks anywhere, it's like they are ghosts that just float through the air never touching the ground. We left the area so as not to disturb the pups and plan to go back in a few weeks to see if we can see them again or at least find some tracks. He said, "it gives "'the Spirit of the Red Wolf' a special meaning."

Sloppy said the cave may hold something special, and Alan thought so too.

Yano sat listening to his elders, understanding and believing more and more about 'The Spirit of the Red Wolf'. He's not sure why, but finding the Wolf pups seemed more important now than finding gold. The next day Yano sat and talked more with Sloppy about his forty years of living in the mountains alone. Yano was very intrigued to hear Sloppy's experiences and stories. He told Sloppy he wanted to be a mountain man and live off the land he had proved he could do it.

Sloppy said, "going on an adventure for a few days and surviving was good and does prove you know how to make it for a few days, but living that lifestyle for years alone is a different story. You need to learn all you can with your education, learn how to do other jobs, and continue learning how to trap, hunt and fish, learn all you can about the mountains and what they can provide if you know where to look, respect the land and its wildlife, love and protect your family and go on your exploring adventures when you can, maybe for just short periods of time then you can come home. I don't have any family, but you do."

Yano was hearing the same things from Sloppy that his father had told him all his young life. He still wanted to go on his adventures, but he listened to his elders and would try to do as they said.

At the supper table Sunday evening, the whole family and Sloppy were enjoying deer tenderloin, biscuits and gravy fried potatoes with onions, and green beans.

Sloppy looked at Yano and said, "you don't have meals like this living as a mountain man."

Yano loved a good meal, and he understood exactly what Sloppy meant by saying that.

Alan said he would have to catch the train in the morning to go to Rockford to work and would not be back home until Wednesday evening.

Sloppy knew that Alan did not want him to leave until he got back. Sloppy said he probably wouldn't head back to his place until Thursday or Friday and asked if he could take the other wagon that Alan used to haul his supplies in when he went to town, he knew the children would use the buckboard for school.

Alan said, "Of course you can."

Sloppy said, "That way, I won't have to pack any of my supplies on my mule until I get ready to go."

Awakened by the rooster crowing, it was Monday morning, and everybody was up doing their chores. After breakfast, Yano, Koda and Ayita took the buckboard to school. Alan was at the train station headed to Rockford. Sloppy was sitting in the shanty drinking coffee by the warmth of the wood stove resting his aching leg before he headed to town to get supplies.

Odina and their youngest daughter, Nokomis were in the house getting ready for homeschooling.

About an hour later, Sloppy hooked his mule up to Alan's wagon. He asked Odina what supplies they needed; he could get them while he was in town.

She gave him a list and told him Alan would pay him when he returned on Wednesday.

Sloppy smiled at her and headed off to town with several ounces of gold he hoped Beanstalk would buy from him. He intended to pay for all the things Odina had on her list to help repay them for all they had done for him. Sloppy had ten ounces of gold and Beanstalk paid him one hundred and eighty dollars for it. Next, he went next door to Liam Dobbs General Store to get all the food supplies. With all the supplies loaded in the wagon, he rode down to the livery stable to get feed for his horse and mule. Even after all he had purchased, he still had a good bit of money left, so he went back to the Trading Post. He was interested in buying two guns that he saw there. He was thinking about one pistol and one rifle he wanted to get for Yano, if Alan approved. If he didn't approve of it right now, maybe he would keep them at their home until he felt it was time for him to have his own guns. Sloppy bought a Colt forty-five caliber Revolver, and a forty-five caliber muzzle loading rifle with a shorter barrel than the fifty caliber Hawkins Rifle that Alan had. Sloppy was excited about his purchase and hoped Alan would allow Yano to have them as gifts, if not at this time, they would be good to have in the house for added protection. He stopped by Roosters Tavern for a shot of whiskey before heading back. While in the Tavern, Sloppy spotted a shady looking character sitting at a table in the corner drinking a beer. The man was Indian, wearing tattered clothing and had a big scar on his face that went from the bottom of the eye to the corner of his mouth. He had all the signs of a man being expelled from his clan.

Sloppy asked Rooster if he knew the man.

Rooster said, "No, he just walked in here and started bugging my customers to buy him a drink. I was about to run him off when Ole Jed over there said he would buy him a beer, but he needed to sit in the corner, because he smelled so bad. His horse is outside with his gear strapped on the saddle. I've never seen him before, and he looks like he's been living in the wild for some time."

Sloppy says, "There is something about him that doesn't sit well with me and if he has been expelled from his clan, it means that he has done something terribly wrong. The scar on his face was marked to show his wrongdoing." Sloppy paid for his shot of whiskey and left, looking at the Indian as he went out the door. Getting on the wagon to head back, he could see the strangers' horse and it looked as bad as he did. The hooves were in bad shape and the horse was unbrushed and loaded down with all kinds of gear. He left, but still had a funny feeling about this guy. Sloppy was very good at reading the signs from animals and people and this guy seemed to be part animal.

He got back to the shanty before the children returned home from school. He hid the firearms in the shanty until Alan returned. When the children got home a few minutes later, they helped unload all the supplies from the wagon. He sat on the porch of the shanty with a cup of coffee watching the three youngest play and he could tell by watching them, they had the urge to explore just like Yano did. He could see Yano walking to him, and he enjoyed talking with Yano and he had something to tell him he didn't want to say in front of anyone else. He asked Yano if he remembered what he told him about the chair tree's location where he retrieved the rope for him.

Yano said, "yes, he remembered."

Sloppy then said, "when I die, go to the top of that ridge with a rope and repel about twenty feet down staying in line with the chair tree and look for something out of place. I will go ahead and tell you there is a wooden box buried there where something is out of place for that location. Inside the wooden box will be a letter from me telling about the contents of the box and the reason your name was written on the letter. I want you to remember three things. Number 1, don't go there until I'm dead, Number 2, don't tell anybody what I've told you and, Number 3, Remember this is the place where I fell, so be careful. Now when I say, 'don't tell anybody, I don't mean your father, I would prefer you told him after I die. He has to know, and you should not go alone.

Chapter 14

Koda and Ayita were playing a game called 'Find Me'. One would hide and the other would wait several minutes, then try to track the other, which helped them with their tracking skills. Little Nokomis was busy swinging on the tree swing Alan had made. Sloppy and Yano were sitting on the porch at the shanty when Sloppy noticed a lone rider going north on Three Bears Trail down below them and he was pretty sure the lone rider was the shady character he saw at Rooster's Tavern. Koda and Ayita were still playing their game, it was Ayita's time to hide from Koda, and she headed off behind the house toward the freshwater spring. When she went to hide, she ran. Koda waited several minutes to start looking for her. Walking slowly trying to find her tracks, he stopped every few feet to listen. It took him longer to get to the freshwater spring because he was walking, and she was running, and she had turned to the left causing him to lose her tracks. Koda continued searching for about thirty minutes and you could hear him calling her name out loud. Calling her name out loud meant he had given up on finding her so she could come out of her hiding place.

Odina heard Koda calling Ayita and went out to Koda, Odina also began calling for her daughter.

Sloppy could sense something was wrong and had a sick feeling in his stomach after seeing the shady character riding north on Three Bears Trail. He told Yano to go to his mother and see what was going on. When Yano reached his mother and brother, Sloppy saddled up Ole Topper to help search by horseback, since he still had trouble walking any distance. Sloppy picked up Nokomis from the swing and handed her to Odina. When he met up with Odina, Yano and Koda, Ayita's tracks indicated she had circled to the left and was traveling toward the bottom land and Three Bears Trail. If she were running the whole distance, she could have made it to Three Bears Trail about the same time that Indian with the bad scar crossed her path. Sloppy continued tracking her by horseback with Odina and the three children following on foot. He could see Ayita's tracks where she crossed the bottom land, and he was hoping she was just going to

Three Bears Trail and turning left to come back to the house and couldn't hear them calling for her.

When Sloppy reached Three Bears Trail, he spotted a little leather pouch with a fancy design sewn on it and recognized it as Ayita's. She would put pretty rocks in it and tie it to her belt. He got off his horse and could see the tracks of a horse with the damaged hooves, then tracks of a man that was made when he got off the horse. Sloppy then saw Ayita's tracks and drag marks there, like she had been dragged to the horse by the man. He knew now that she had been taken by the man with the bad scar on his face and they had about an hour's head start.

Odina and the children came to where Sloppy was and she could tell by the look on his face something bad had happened to Ayita.

Sloppy said, "I know who this is that has taken Ayita. I don't know his name, but I saw him today at Roosters Tavern. He's an Indian that looked to have been expelled from his clan, he had a bad scar on his face from the bottom of his eye to the corner of his mouth. These are the tracks from his horse, it has damaged hooves.

Odina, with a nervous quiver in her voice walked up closer to Sloppy so the children couldn't hear and said, "that scar was put on a person that had committed something bad to a child in their village. We must find her quickly, she's in terrible danger."

Sloppy said he would go now while he still had some light to see the tracks. "You and the children go back to the house."

Yano spoke up and said he wanted to go too, "she's my sister and I can help."

Odina agreed, "Yes take Yano with you, he can help you track them." She went back to the house and put some food in a bag for them to take while Yano saddled up Smokie.

Sloppy said, "okay," and told Yano, "Look under the bunk in the shanty and grab the new rifle and pistol and bring them along, also bring the cloth bag that has ammunition for both firearms and grab a couple of extra blankets and canteens of water too." Sloppy told Odina to go into town and tell the marshal what had happened and tell him it was the Indian with the scar on his face that took Ayita. "You will also need to send a telegraph to

Rockford and have them get in touch with Alan, so he can get back here as soon as possible. "Me and Yano will head north on Three Bears Trail, and we will mark our path with an X mark on the ground if we get off Three Bears Trail and other places, so they will know which way we are going." Sloppy told them to hurry and get the supplies ready, "they had an hour head start already. When he grabbed Ayita, they left running, but he felt that horse couldn't run too far in the shape it was in when he saw it."

Yano was loaded up and back to Sloppy in five minutes and they left searching for Ayita and the madman.

Odina had Koda and Nokomis get on her horse, PoGo, with her and would drop them off at the Bolins before she headed to town.

After dropping the children off, Odina rode as hard as she could to get to town. She went straight to the telegraph office and found Wilbur Williams still there. He sent the telegraph to Rockford Virginia to be delivered to Alan Adams at the hotel. It said, *"Get home as soon as possible, daughter has been taken by a stranger."* Odina told Mr. Williams she was going over to the Marshal's Office and if he heard back to please let her know, she needed to know contact with her husband was made.

At the Marshal's Office, she met Deputy Booger Moore and began telling him their daughter had been taken by an Indian with a bad scar on his face. As she was telling him, Marshal McCall walked in, and she explained all she could to both men. Then she told them, their good friend Sloppy had seen the man earlier at Roosters Tavern.

Marshal McCall spoke up and said they both knew Sloppy and remembered seeing the Indian she was speaking of.

She continued telling them she knew what the scar on his face meant, "the man had been expelled from his tribe's clan due to something bad he had done to a young girl. Our daughter Ayita is seven years old and in extreme danger." Odina told them Sloppy was staying with them for a few days and he saw the man riding north on Three Bears Trail, just before we knew that Ayita was missing. Ayita and her twin brother Koda were playing a game called 'Find Me' and Ayita had gone a little further when it was her time to hide and ended up at Three Bears Trail, we found her small leather pouch there and could see marks on the ground where he dragged her to his horse. His horse has damaged hooves and will be easy to track in the light, Sloppy and my oldest son are tracking them now and I have sent a telegraph to my husband, Alan Adams. He's in Rockford, Virginia working at the new coal mine there. She also told the marshal that Sloppy said, "they would leave an X mark on the ground, if the tracks get off Three Bears Trail, then they would make X marks along the way, so you would know it was them." Odina said, "please help us get our daughter back."

Marshal McCall told his deputy to go to Roosters Tavern and see if anyone knew the man, where he came from or where he might be going. He assured Odina they would do everything possible to bring her daughter home, he knew where the Adams' house was on Three Bears Trail, and he would get a posse together and leave out at first light. "We will stop by your house first to see if you have any more information. I have dealt with some crazy mean people in my twenty years as a marshal, but never had a case like this, I can't imagine the fear this little girl is going through."

As Odina was leaving the Marshal's Office, Mr. Williams came running across the street to tell her that Alan had got the message and would catch the next train to Shepherd Springs. Odina was a little relieved knowing Alan would be home with her during this terrible crime committed against their family. It was dark now as she headed back to the Bolins to pick up Koda and Nokomis to go home and wait. When she arrived there, Tehya insisted on going with them to stay and help her. Tehya said, "I was there when each of your children were born, now I will be there when Ayita comes home."

With tears in her eyes, Odina smiled and said, "thank you to Tehya."

Ridge and Lucus wanted to help, they would head out at first light and Ridge asked Odina for all the information she knew about the man that took Ayita.

She told him them all that Sloppy had got a good look at him earlier at Roosters Tavern, he was an Indian that looked like he had been expelled from his tribe's clan for a wrong he had committed and had been living in the wild for some time. He also had a bad scar on his face from the bottom of his eye to the corner of his mouth. When Odina spoke of the scar, Tehya gave her a worried look, but didn't say anything, she knew what the scar meant. "Sloppy said his horse looked in bad shape too and had damaged hooves which made it easy to track in daylight. We found Ayita's little leather pouch on the trail where he grabbed her. Horse tracks by a horse with damaged hooves were there also and marks on the ground where he dragged her to his horse."

Odina told Ridge and Lucas that Sloppy and Yano started tracking them about two hours before dark and said they would make an X mark on the ground if they broke off Three Bears Trail, then they would leave an X mark every once in a while, so anybody following them would know it was them.

Ridge thanked Odina for the information on the man's description and about the horse's damaged hooves.

Odina, Koda, Nokomis and Tehya left to go their house and wait for some news. When they arrived at their house, Tehya took her and Odina's horse to the pasture while Odina put her children to bed, then she built a fire in the fireplace for her and Tehya to sit by while they waited.

At one point, Odina stepped outside, looked up to the stars, and prayed to her God for Ayita's safe return and for the safety of Yano and Sloppy and all the other searchers. There would be no sleep for these friends as they talked about the events that happened today. Odina told Tehya that when she talked of the scar on the man's face, she could tell by looking at her that she knew what it meant. Then she asked Tehya what tribe she thought this mad man belonged to.

Tehya said, "the Shawnee Tribe, but not anymore. The elders gave him that mark on his face, so no one would ever want him as a mate, then they forced him to leave the Tribe, never to return. He was probably from a Shawnee Tribe just east of the Mississippi River and traveled this far east to escape the treatment he would receive if seen again in their area. He will always be on the run, hiding out in the mountains and staying away from people except when he feels the need to take something from somebody."

Sloppy and Yano had been traveling in the dark now and had to slow down almost to a crawl in order to see the tracks of the horse with the damaged hooves. They heard horses coming towards them and as they got closer, they could tell it was two riders. They waited with caution, Sloppy pulled his pistol out and held it down by his side, he told Yano to do the same with the Colt forty-five caliber pistol and if he saw these two men go for their guns to shoot them.

The two riders stopped when they got to Sloppy and Yano and said, "howdy."

Sloppy spoke back and asked where they were heading.

One of the men said Shepherd Springs to the coal mine there, they were looking for work and heard they might need coal miners there or at a new mine in Rockford.

Sloppy was pretty sure these men meant them no harm and asked them if they had seen anybody on this trail going north.

One man said, "Yes, about two or three hours ago, we met one horse that had two people on it, a grown man with a kid, they looked Indian, but cut off the trail before we got close enough to talk to them.”

Sloppy asked which way they went when they got off the trail.

The man doing all the talking said west in the direction of the Potomac River.

“Did the kid look okay?” Sloppy asked.”

The man said he wasn’t close enough to tell, he just thought it was a father and his kid because they were on one horse riding together. “Are you looking for those two people?”

Sloppy said, “Yes, we are, what did the area look like where you last saw them?”

The man said, “there were large boulders that would be on your right going north and where they went off the trail was thick timber sloping down to a meadow. It was already pretty dark, but we could see that much.”

Sloppy bid the men good luck on their search for a job in coal mining, but they probably would need to go to Rockford because the mine in Shepherd Springs was on the verge of closing down.

The men thanked him and continued south on Three Bears Trail.

Sloppy and Yano continued north.

Chapter 15

It was five thirty Tuesday morning, Odina and Tehya heard a horse galloping up the path to the house. They both rushed to the front door hoping it was good news. It was Alan and he had fire in his eyes, Odina had never seen him angry, and Alan had never seen Odina this worried. Odina told Alan that it was Ayita that the man took. She gave Alan the bad man's description, "he was Indian, and he had a bad scar on his face from his eye to his mouth, his horse had damaged hooves you could tell by its tracks. They believe he had been expelled from his Tribal clan and the scar was a mark they gave him for the wrong he had committed." She said, "Sloppy and Yano started tracking them yesterday, a few hours before dark. Sloppy said he would leave an X mark on the ground if they got off the trail and then leave them throughout their journey so he would know it was them. The tracks were going north on Three Bears Trail. Sloppy had seen him earlier in Roosters Tavern, then again going north on Three Bears Trail down in front of their house. About one hour later, was when they discovered Ayita missing. She and Koda were playing their game of 'Find Me' and she ended up down at the trail. We found her leather pouch and saw drag marks on the ground where he grabbed her.

Alan said, "Okay, we will find her, and he will pay for this crime."

Tehya had gathered up some deer jerky and flat bread and put it in a cloth bag for him to take with him, they both knew he would not come back until he found Ayita. With no sleep, Alan left in the dark. Tehya's two sons, Ridge and Lucus rode up thirty minutes later just to check in and see if they had heard anything. They had already been briefed on descriptions and knew that Sloppy and Yano and now Alan were out searching, so they took off to help.

At daybreak, Marshal McCall and two deputized men stopped by the Adams' house to advise Odina that he had sent three more telegraphs. One to Linnville, Virginia, one to Locust Springs, Virginia and one to High Point, Virginia. The telegrams advised the law in those towns to be on the lookout for an Indian with a bad scar on his face. He was wanted for abducting a seven-year-old girl and if located detain him and send a telegraph to Marshal

McCall in Shepherd Springs, Virginia to arrange for the safe return of the seven-year-old girl named Ayita Adams. Odina also made them aware of all the men that were now out tracking the mad man.

It was daylight when Sloppy and Yano found the tracks where they left the trail. Sloppy marked an X on the ground as they continued tracking in the big timber and through a meadow going west. Sloppy and Yano had not slept and neither had the mad man that had Ayita. There are now eight men tracking and searching for this Indian that had taken Ayita. Riding west for about two more hours, Yano noticed the Indian's tracks turned north. Sloppy marked the spot with an X and they continued riding north. Sloppy knew if the crazy Indian didn't let his horse rest, it would probably fall over dead. He could tell it was walking now, not running as much, so maybe they could gain some ground on them.

The temperature was warming up after a cold night. Sloppy and Yano came to a creek and decided to give the horses a much-needed break and give them time to eat a bite. Sloppy put an X mark on the ground at this location. The leg Sloppy broke was healed, but was causing him a lot of pain, so he walked around a little hoping to ease it some. After resting for about five minutes, they were back in the saddle again when they heard someone coming, they were on high alert until they could see it was Alan. After it got daylight, Alan could see the tracks of the horse with damaged hooves well and Sloppy and Yano's tracks also. He rode Scout pretty hard after it got light and spotted every X mark on the ground that Sloppy had made. Alan told Sloppy and Yano that Tehya's sons, Ridge and Lucus were coming to help, and Marshal McCall said he would deputize a couple more men and join the search, Odina said, all of them had been told of the Indian's scar on his face and the damaged hooves on his horse. They would also know of the X marks on the ground Sloppy left so they would know it was them.

Alan looked at Sloppy and said, "You don't look so good Sloppy."

Sloppy said, "I'm okay, just some pain in his leg that was broken."

Alan said, "Why don't you stay here until the other help arrives, build you a fire and rest some while I go on with Yano, while we have good light to track by."

Sloppy agreed, but said, "as soon as the help gets here, we are coming after you."

Alan said he would continue to leave an X mark on the ground to let him know they were still finding the damaged hoof prints. He then noticed Yano had a revolver and a rifle and asked where he got those guns. Before Yano could answer, Sloppy spoke up and told him they were his, "I felt Yano should have some protection on this trip and you know how well Yano can shoot and how safe he was. I hope that was alright?"

Alan said, "Yes, it it's okay and thank you Sloppy."

Before Alan and Yano left, Sloppy told Alan about seeing this man in Roosters Tavern and he could sense danger just by the way he acted, then he saw the same man and his horse going north on Three Bears Trail in front of the house. A little later was when they discovered Ayita was missing. "When you see him, you will know him because of the scar on his face."

Alan and Yano left at a pretty good pace hoping to gain some ground on the bad man that has his daughter. He promised Odina he would bring Ayita home. They needed to travel all the distance they could while it was light enough to see the tracks, after dark it would be walking speed and take a long time to gain any distance.

Ridge and Lucus made it to Sloppy's location about forty-five minutes after Alan and Yano had left. They took a quick break and said, "let's go."

Sloppy told them to wait a little longer because Marshal McCall should be coming also with some help.

Marshal McCall and his two deputies got to Sloppy's location about twenty minutes after Ridge and Lucas.

After talking for a few minutes. Sloppy said, "Let's get going and try to catch up with Alan and Yano before dark. Once we are all together, we can come up with a plan of action. We can then decide if we want to split up or all stay together, there are hundreds of miles of rough terrain to cover and the speed we do it in is very important for Ayita's safety."

They had no problem following the tracks left by Alan and Yano and could also still see the tracks from the damaged hooves that the bad man was leaving.

Back at the Adams' home, Tehya's daughter, Nova had come up to help with Koda and Nokomis and her husband, Clyde, came to do any chores that needed to be done.

Odina was so thankful to have such neighbors. Tehya tried to get her to sleep, but she couldn't, all Odina could think about was *how frightened Ayita was not understanding what was going on. Is she harmed, is she hungry, is she cold or is she in shock?* All these things were going through her mind and all she could do was pray and ask God to protect her daughter and bring her home.

Darkness had fallen for the second night and Sloppy, Ridge, Lucus, Marshal McCall and his two deputies had just caught up with Alan and Yano. Sloppy could not understand why they had not caught up with the bad man because he saw what kind of shape his horse was in. Even though he had about two hours head start on them, his horse couldn't have run for too long at a time. As all eight men that are searching for Ayita gathered around, Alan spoke of a plan to better utilize the eight searchers instead of all being clumped together. Alan thought he should go alone slowly following the tracks, Sloppy and Yano would stay there, and rest for two to three hours, then follow him in case he circled back between them. He would like Ridge and Lucas to go west a couple of miles then turn north. He would like Marshal McCall and his two deputies to go east until they came to Three Bears Trail and then go north for a couple of miles, then turn and go west. "Should any of you see the damaged hoof tracks, mark the ground with an X. Keep your eyes and ears on alert and look for a campfire, I'm sure even the crazy man is cold. If any of you find Ayita and the bad man is dead or has been captured and tied up, fire three shots in the air, wait one minute, then fire three more shots. Sound travels a long way in the mountains, especially at night. Also, if you find a camp, don't ride up on your horses, go by foot and sneak up on him. Remember, this animal probably hears things better than we do, so you have to be quiet. If anyone finds Ayita and fires three shots, then three more shots, the other groups should fire one shot to show you heard the three shots and three more shots and are coming to that area."

Marshal McCall agreed with Alan's plans, knowing that this way would form a perimeter, then eventually they should all be close to connecting again.

Alan knew he could make better time going alone and wouldn't make as much noise as a group would make.

The bad man was probably thinking nobody was following him, so he stopped riding and built a fire to warm by. He had Ayita tied up, so she couldn't run away and kept telling her in a language that was not Cherokee, that she belonged to him and would do as he said. He spoke broken English, but she had a hard time understanding what he was saying and what he was going to do with her. She was frightened, cold, hungry and missing her family. She didn't know if she would ever see them again.

The bad man took out his knife and stuck it to the fire as Ayita watched in fear. Then the bad man took a piece of cloth and gagged Ayita with it. With the blade of the knife red hot, he burned a mark on Ayita's face, to match his scar, from the bottom of her eye to the corner of her mouth. She screamed in pain, but her sound didn't go out because of the gag in her mouth. He looked her in the eyes with his evil eyes and repeated that she belonged to him as he pointed to his scar then to hers. He had her tied up and lying on the ground under a rock ledge close to the fire. He draped a deer hide over her little body and laid on the ground next to her and covered up with a dirty old blanket that smelled as bad as he did. In about five minutes, Ayita could hear him snoring and she tried to untie the knots on the rope, but was unable to. Ayita didn't know that her father, brother, Sloppy, neighbors Ridge and Lucas, and the marshal with two deputies were searching for her. She did know that her mother knew she was missing and was probably looking for her, *but how will they know where she is?*

She didn't even know where she was, but she did know it had been two long days since she had seen her family.

Chapter 16

It was early night, and the moon was full which helped Alan see the damaged hoof tracks better. He traveled up and around large boulders. All the crevices and large boulders made for a good ambush point, so Alan stayed on alert. If this bad man knew he was being followed, he might try to eliminate the threat by ambushing them. Alan got off Scout and climbed up on top of one of the boulders looking for a fire and listening for any human sounds. He was discouraged, but would never give up on finding his seven-year-old daughter Ayita.

Sloppy and Yano had both fallen asleep from pure exhaustion which is exactly what Alan wanted them to do. His old friend did not look well to him, and he wanted his son to stay safe, any contact with this bad man would be bad and he didn't want Yano getting hurt or killed, plus he knew he could make better time alone and be the quietest with only one horse. Alan walked Scout in the dark while he was tracking, so he could see the ground better and to remove his body weight from Scout because he knew he was tired too.

It was bitter cold with the wind blowing through the valleys and as long as he went slow, he could still see the tracks well enough. Just as he tracked around the base of a mountain, the wind stopped blowing and the mountains were completely silent. Alan stopped and listened, sounds travel a long way in the mountains at night, but it was hard to pinpoint the location of whatever sounds you heard. After standing there for about five minutes, resting and listening, he heard the undeniable sound of a Wolf howling. It sounded like it came from about two mountains over from where he was. Alan knew it was tricky to locate exactly where the sound came from, but he moved in the direction he believed was its location. He had been walking and riding slowly for hours and thought he had only an hour of darkness left, he picked up his pace. To him, the location of the howling Wolf was where his treasure could be found, and Ayita was his treasure. He was still seeing the damaged hoof prints as he went around the base of the second mountain. He could smell the smoke from a campfire. Alan saw the flicker of flames from a campfire about two hundred yards straight across this valley and halfway up on the side of the mountain. He tied Scout to a tree, took his Hawkins Rifle out of the scabbard with plenty of ammo for it and his forty-four-caliber pistol and quietly sneaked up to within forty yards of this camp. He could tell someone was lying on the ground behind the fire that was bigger than Ayita. He didn't see her, so he wasn't sure if this bad man had killed her and dumped her somewhere or if this was really the bad man lying on the ground. He eased up a little closer and spotted a horse that looked in bad shape like Sloppy said. Then the man lying on the ground got up, threw more wood on the fire and stood with his back to the fire. With the fire causing more light, he could see what he believed to be a deer hide draped over something under a rock ledge and a few yards from where the man was standing. The man turned to warm his front and Alan, for the first time saw his face. He had a bad scar right where Sloppy said. He could even smell the bad body odor of this man, but where was his Ayita? Alan had his fifty caliber Hawkins Rifle sights on the man's chest when he noticed the movement of the deer hide under the rock ledge. He knew that it was his daughter, and this was the bad man that took her.

Alan yelled at the man, telling him to put his hands up. The startled man looked in Alan's direction with a wild look in his eyes and drew his revolver. Just as the bad man was pointing it in Alan's direction, Alan squeezed the trigger on the fifty-caliber rifle striking the bad man in the chest. Falling backwards the Indian was yelling, "M'… WaWi… M' WaWi," that was how the Shawnee said wolf. Apparently, the bad man had also heard the howling of the Wolf and knew it gave his location away. Alan ran up to the bad man, took his pistol and the long gun laying on the ground. The Indian was not dead yet, but he would be. Alan then ran over to the deer hide and uncovered a tied up and frightened little girl. The first thing he noticed was the bad mark on her face, but it was Ayita, she was alive and now she was safe. He untied her and hugged her, to help get her warm. Alan was so angry at the animal that took his daughter and scared her face that he dragged the man's body over to the fire and stuck both his feet in the fire, so he could feel some more pain before he stopped breathing. The man did die a few seconds after that.

Ayita told her father she didn't think anybody was going to find her. Alan told his daughter that he promised himself and her mother he would bring her back. "I'm so sorry Ayita that I couldn't get her sooner and I am sorry you had to experience this evil act, but you have shown how strong you really are, and I am so very proud of you. We have seven more people up here searching for you including your brother, Yano, and I need to send a signal by firing three shots, then three more again to let them know I found you. After I fire all six shots, you listen for a single shot, if they can hear my six shots, there should be three single shots from three different locations."

Not knowing for sure if they were able to hear his fifty-caliber shot or not, he took out his pistol and fired three shots in the air, waited a minute, then fired three more and listened. He heard a single shot to his east that sounded close, then he heard a single shot to his south and then a single shot to his west. He was happy everybody heard his shots, and they should all be on the way to them. Alan dragged the body of the bad man away from the fire, so he could get Ayita closer to warm herself better, he would not have her close to that animal ever again. He had a canteen of water and some jerky in his pocket, so he gave Ayita some. He would still have to go where he tied Scout to a tree, but he would wait for the others to find him. Yano and Sloppy might come by Scout too and bring him. He would keep the fire going even though it was breaking day now, it would help them locate him and Ayita. Alan inspected the wound on her face. Ayita said, "he burned me with his knife, and he said I belonged to him now."

Alan wanted to kill him again. "You do not belong to him, never did and never will." Alan asked her if she was hurt anywhere else and she said, "No, Father, he let me drink a little water, but I never had any food."

They could hear horses coming, so Alan took Ayita and they both got behind a rock until they knew for sure who it was coming to them.

Marshal McCall called out, "Hello in the camp"

Alan recognized it was Marshal McCall's voice and answered, "Over here Marshal."

The marshal and his two deputies rode into the camp with a relieved happiness on their face when they saw Ayita sitting there alive. The marshal walked over to the dead man, inspected his wound and noticed his feet being burnt. Marshal McCall walked back over to Alan and said, "You know I'm the U.S. Marshal for this territory and am sworn to uphold the law and report all deaths that are not of natural causes."

Alan said, "I understand."

Marshal McCall said. "It looks like this bad man killed himself and when he fell, his feet went into the fire."

Alan called the Marshal off to the side where others couldn't hear them and said, "Marshal, you and I both know this man didn't kill himself, but I must tell you, I gave him a chance to give up, but he drew on me, so I shot him."

The marshal said, "Well that's self-defense and no charges against you will be made." He also said he would take the body to Linville, which was about ten more miles north. He said, "Three Bears Trail goes to Linville and the trail is less than a half a mile east of us here. We had already got off the trail when you fired the signal shots. I'll fill out a report with the Sheriff in Linville and have them bury him face down, so if his spirit tries to dig out, he will dig to hell where he can continue to burn. It's always sad to see some people die, but this would have been terrible to see an animal like this live."

Sloppy and Yano were next to arrive at their location and they had Scout with them. They were both excited to see Ayita. Yano hugged his little sister and told her. "it's over now; you are safe."

Yano took his blanket from his bed roll and wrapped Ayita in it to stay warm.

Marshal McCall and his two deputies loaded the dead man on his own horse that was in bad shape. The marshal told Alan he would send a telegram to all the locations that he had sent them to letting them know that Ayita had been found safe and the bad man that took her had been eliminated. He said, "I will also send word to my deputy in Shepherd Springs to ride out and tell Odina, if that is alright with you, because it would probably take you about two days to get home, and I should be in Linville in less than two hours. We will stay the night in Linville and will stop by your house in a few days when we return."

Alan said, "Thank you, I know Odina is worried sick."

The marshal and his deputies and the dead man rode off and headed north to Linville.

Alan told Yano to let Ayita ride with him, his horse was younger and stronger and could haul more weight than his older Scout could. He asked Sloppy, "Are you able to leave now or do you want to rest a while longer.?"

Sloppy said, "Let's go now, we will probably need to stop and camp one more time on the way back."

Ridge and Lucus were ready to go, so they all left and got on Three Bears Trail and heading south.

Marshal McCall and his deputies arrived in Linville and went straight to the sheriff's office. They met with Sheriff Burton and explained to him that they had a very bad and dead man draped over a poor unhealthy horse out front. The sheriff and marshal knew each other very well and when the sheriff looked at the dead man he told the marshal, "What you have here is a Shawnee Indian that they call Tunga. When I got your telegram the other day, I started asking around town to see if anybody had heard anything of a man like this. There's an old Shawnee Indian that works or hangs around the livery stable that said he had heard of this man. It was said, he was expelled from his Tribes Clan in Mississippi. They gave him a scar on his face for trying to molest a young girl. He was ordered to leave their village and never to return, death would come to him if he was ever seen. He was wanted for killing a young Cherokee girl in North Carolina and for taking and molesting a nine-year-old white girl in north Georgia. She was able to escape from him, but the authorities could not find him. There is a five-hundred-dollar reward for him dead or alive." Sheriff Burton told Marshal McCall he would give the reward money to him.

The marshal said, "Well, he's not wanted anymore, he's dead. I can't accept the reward money for myself or my deputies, but I can take it to the little girl that we just rescued from him that went through two days of pure hell where he burnt a scar on her beautiful face with a hot knife blade."

The sheriff said he would get the undertaker to bury him and would give his horse to the livery stable to see if they could get it healthy again.

McCall said that sounded good, but when you bury him, bury him face down, so hell would be the only way he could go. Now, I need to go to the telegraph office and send a few telegrams that he has been killed and the little girl is on her way home alive and well." The marshal said he would have his deputy in Shepherd Springs ride out and tell Odina Adams that her daughter was on the way home, alive and well.

Chapter 17

At ten thirty Wednesday morning, Deputy Booger Moore rode up to the Adams' house to deliver the news he had just received from Marshal McCall's telegram.

Odina had not slept since Sunday night. She heard a horse riding up their path and with a sick feeling, she came out on the front porch to greet the approaching visitor. She could see it was Deputy Moore and he appeared to be smiling. She got a feeling of relief just seeing him smile.

Deputy Moore, without hesitation, told her that Ayita was safe and, on her way, home.

Odina fell to her knees with tears of joy and gave thanks to her God for answering her prayers.

Deputy Moore told her that it would probably be some time tomorrow before they got home. He thought she was found close to Linville and the telegram said *the bad man is no longer a threat to anyone ever again, he's dead.*

Odina had a lot of questions, but Deputy Moore did not know the answers. She would have to wait until Alan got home with their daughter.

Tehya was standing on the porch behind Odina when Deputy Moore delivered the good news. She hugged Odina, and said, "the nightmare is over."

Odina was so exhausted she could hardly stand or speak, but she said, "Thank you," to Deputy Moore for delivering the wonderful news.

Linville was fifty-five miles up Three Bears Trail, north of Shepherd Springs.

Alan, Ayita, Yano, Sloppy, Ridge and Lucus would try and make a shelter to get out of the cold and camp one night, so all of them could rest and rest the horses. They should make it home Thursday, probably around lunch.

After riding all day and being awake for three days, Alan said they needed to stop and build a lean to and shelter from the cold as best they could. He could see a stream up ahead with a lot of limbs on the ground that they could use and also burn for heat. The horses could get water from the stream. They built a fire first and wrapped Ayita up in a blanket to stay warm by the fire.

Alan told Sloppy to sit with Ayita while the rest of them built a quick shelter. They had a shelter built in a short time and had removed the saddles from the horses, let them get water, then tied all of them to a rope stretched between two trees. Next, they did a food inventory. Alan and Yano still had plenty of deer jerky and flatbread. Ridge and Lucus had more of the same in their saddlebags. They divided the food up as they sat around the fire and ate. This shelter could be seen from the trail, Alan thought Marshal McCall and his deputies might want to use it too, when they came through.

Alan was up before light and so were Ridge and Lucus. They stoked the fire and saddled all their horses. Soon as Ayita, Yano and Sloppy got up, they would leave.

Everybody was up now and eating a little more flatbread and jerky. Alan and Sloppy were sure wishing they had some coffee to drink, but didn't bring any. That was okay with them though, because they had Ayita and would be home in a few more hours. They would make better time going back because they wouldn't be looking for the damaged hoof tracks.

Alan kept his eye on Ayita. He knew the burn on her face was painful, but she didn't cry or complain. He had some bear grease at home that should help that burn heal and he would get Dr. Hogue or Dr. Clark to come out and check on her.

It seemed they had been riding forever, but at 11:00A.M. they arrived at the Adams' house.

Odina ran down the path to meet them with Koda, Nokomis and Tehya following her. Odina grabbed Ayita from Yano's horse and hugged her. She got an angry look on her face when she saw the burn on Ayita's face. *How could a person do such an evil thing to a child?* She reassured Ayita that everything would be alright now, "You are home and safe and we will take care of that burn."

Ayita smiled at her mother and said, "I'm sorry Mother for running down to the trail and letting that crazy man take me away."

Odina said, "It's not your fault Child, and you have nothing to apologize for, it is I that should apologize for not looking out for you better." Odina looked at Alan and said, "Put the horses in the pasture and come eat some warm food and drink some coffee."

Tehya had made a large pot of pea soup with ham and onions in it and, also, some corn fritters.

Odina carried Ayita to the house, cleaned her face and put some bear grease on her burn. All the men came and gathered around the table to enjoy a hot meal and coffee. Before they started, Alan said grace over the wonderful meal that sat on the table and told the Lord how thankful they were for the friendship and help his friends gave without question and most of all, they were thankful that they found Ayita alive and brought her home.

Alan would tell Odina all about this long search later when nobody else was around. Right now, they just wanted to enjoy being home with family and friends.

After they finished eating, Ridge and Lucus Bolin went home.

Sloppy said he was going to the shanty, and with a little laugh, said, "I'll probably sleep for two days."

Odina would help bathe Ayita and put her to bed. Tehya said she would watch the children so Odina could finally lay down and sleep. Alan said he would ride PoGo into town and see if Dr. Hogue or Dr. Clark could ride out and examine Ayita for any other injuries.

Yano spoke up and said, "I'll go."

Alan said, "Thank you Yano, I know you would, but I need to go, so I can send a telegram to Mr. Stockburn in Rockford. You stay here, take care of our family and rest yourself."

When Alan was riding into town, he met Nova Bolin on the trail. She said she was going to their house to let her mother come home and rest. Nova said she would watch over Koda and Nokomis while everybody was resting. Alan thanked her and said he knew Tehya was exhausted, she had stayed awake this whole entire time with Odina and had done so much for us as all of you have.

When Alan got to Dr. Hogue's office, Dr. Hogue was there, but not Dr. Clark. Dr. Hogue said he heard about Ayita being taken and then that she was found, but never heard of her condition. "How is she Alan?"

Alan said, "She appears to be okay, but the bad man burned her on her face, and we would like you or Dr.

Clark to check her out and, also, see if you have something better for a burn that bear grease."

Dr. Hogue said, "Bear grease is good, but I have something that will help eliminate the scarring." Dr. Hogue was in his late seventies now and said he would come out in a few. Dr. Clark was out seeing patients on the other side of town.

Alan said, "Thanks Doc, I really appreciate it and I will see you there, but first, I need to get a telegram sent to Rockford to let my boss know Ayita has been found and we got her home safe."

Dr. Hogue arrived at the Adams' home about an hour later, after talking with Alan. He asked Odina to stay in the room with him as he examined her. He took a small jar out of his black bag and handed it to Odina. He said, "The bear grease is good, but this salve is better, it has mink oil in it which will help to eliminate scarring. Twice a day, I want you to cover the burn with this salve, but don't bandage it and keep it clean. No playing in the dirt Ayita for a couple of weeks." Dr. Hogue motioned for Odina to step outside the room and with Alan standing there too, he told them that he didn't see any sign of her being molested, but the mark on her face probably meant to him that she was his property. "I hope the SOB is dead for doing that to her."

Alan was a little shocked, he had never heard Dr. Hogue use that kind of language before, but he assured him that the evil animal was dead and buried face down, so he could continue to burn in hell.

Dr. Hogue told them that he wanted to check on her again in a week to see how it was healing. He said Ayita was so young that there may not be much scarring when she gets older, just apply that salve twice a day for about two weeks, then we will check again and may apply it once a day for a while. Dr. Hogue shook his head and said he didn't understand how anyone could harm a child, but it could have been a lot worse if you hadn't found her when you did.

Chapter 18

Alan asked Dr. Hogue if he would check on Sloppy before he left and said, "he is down at the shanty down at the barn. Sloppy had said that the leg that he broke a year ago was causing him a lot of pain."

Dr. Hogue said, "Yes," so Alan went with him to the shanty.

Sloppy was lying down, but not asleep. Dr. Hogue talked with Sloppy and examined his leg. His leg was swollen, and he had some pain when he stood on it or walked too much.

Dr. Hogue said, "It's arthritis, you will always have pain in that leg, but you can ease the pain by wrapping your leg in a warm compress, then rotate by wrapping a cold wet cloth around your leg for about ten minutes. It's time consuming and won't heal or cure the arthritis, but will relieve the pain for short periods of time. My advice is to stay off of it for a few days as much as you can. Rest will help some. I know you have had a hard three days. I will check back in a week when he came back to check on Ayita." It was getting late in the day now and Dr. Hogue left.

Alan brought Sloppy more firewood in the shanty and they talked a little more about their experience. Alan told Sloppy he was glad that he was there when this happened and sorry he wasn't. Alan could tell Sloppy was feeling bad about what happened because of what he could see in the bad man when he first saw him.

Sloppy spoke up and said, "I should have gotten up and followed him when I saw him going up Three Bears Trail."

Alan said, "You had no idea that Ayita had run down to the trail, as far as you knew, the kids were playing behind the house. If it wasn't for you Sloppy, we may not have ever found her. You gave the description of the man and of his horse having damaged hooves that made it easier to track, so I thank you my friend, we are forever in your debt. I'll have Yano bring you some more of that pea soup in a few hours. You have plenty of coffee, water and firewood for now, so just stay off that leg as much as you can."

Sloppy smiled at Alan and says, "Yes Sir, that soup was mighty good, I'll just stay here and rest a while."

All the livestock had been taken care of; Alan walked back up to the house. Ayita was laying down in her bed. Odina was in her bed, Yano was in his bed resting and Nova was playing a game with Koda and Nokomis in front of the fireplace. Alan told Nova, "You can go home now; I can watch the children until bedtime. Everybody should be rested by tomorrow and hopefully things will get back to normal. Alan told Nova, "Thanks for everything that you've done, it means a lot for us to have good friends and neighbors like all of you. If you or any of your family ever needs us for anything, we will be there for y'all just like y'all are always here for us."

Nova smiled as she was leaving, she turned and said, "I can remember more than once when you and Odina helped our family, we love all of you and are happy Ayita is home safe."

It was almost suppertime, and everybody was up. Odina started heating the large pot of pea soup that Tehya had made for them. There was plenty enough to feed the family one more time. There was also a basket full of corn fritters. Tehya made sure they had plenty to eat.

Yano asked his father if they had to go to school in the morning.

Alan said "No, you and Koda can wait until Monday to go back. Ayita will probably need to stay out another week. We will send a note explaining your absence. Alan told Yano to take Sloppy a bowl full of pea soup with some corn fritters. Dr. Hogue told him to stay off that leg for a while, so I don't want him walking to get up here."

After supper, all the children went to bed early. Alan and Odina sat in their rocking chairs in front of the fireplace drinking coffee. He told her about this ordeal and how much everyone helped search for their daughter. "When I caught up with Yano and Sloppy, I made Sloppy stay there and wait on the others you told me were coming, while me and Yano kept going. Sloppy didn't look so good and his leg was hurting, so I wanted him to rest. They could find us when they all showed up. At night, we had to walk slowly just to see the tracks. Once it got dark, we could hear them coming to us. When we were all gathered together, I came up with a plan to split up and I would go alone. I told Ridge and Lucas to go west two miles then turn north. I told Marshal McCall and his two deputies to go east until they hit Three Bears Trail, then go north. I knew I could be quieter and make better time alone. I advised Yano and Sloppy to wait three or four hours then follow me in case the bad man tried to circle back. I said if anybody finds them and the bad man is captured or dead, fire six shots in the air and hope everyone hears the shots. If you heard the shots, you are to fire one shot to show you heard it and you are on your way. It was probably an hour before daylight, I had stopped to listen, the wind was blowing making it difficult to hear, then the wind just stopped.

It was at that time I heard the howling of a Wolf. It sounded like it was two mountains from me. I just knew I had to go toward that sound. After about thirty minutes, I could see the light of a campfire up on the side of a mountain a few hundred yards away. I tied Scout to a tree and walked until I got close to the campfire. I had to sneak closer to see a figure larger than Ayita laying on the ground behind the fire. I could not see Ayita, but I did see what looked like a deer hide draped over something under a rock ledge to the right of the large figure laying on the ground. *Could I be wrong? Have I been tracking the wrong person? Is this the location of the howling of the Wolf? Is this the bad man lying there? If it is, where is my daughter? What if it is him and has my daughter hid out somewhere? Do I rush in and take the chance? The tracks I had been following led me here. The location of the howling Wolf is what I truly believed to be right here.* Just then, the man got up, threw more wood on the fire which lite up the area more, I still couldn't see Ayita or this man's face. I could tell he was Indian, but he had his back to me. Then he turned around to warm by the fire and now I could see his face with a big scar on it. Then I noticed movement under that deer hide a few yards to the right and I knew that it had to be Ayita under it. From about twenty yards, I centered my sights from my fifty caliber Hawkins Rifle on his chest, he still didn't know I was there. I could see a sidearm on his right side. I yelled out for him to raise his hands. Instead of doing that, he drew his weapon and pointed it in my direction. I squeezed the trigger and fired, striking him in the chest.

As he was falling back, he yelled, "M'Wa Wi… M'Wa Wi, two times."

Odina spoke up and said, "wolf, he was calling out wolf in Shawnee."

Alan said, "I guess he heard the howling of the Wolf too. I ran up to him and removed his pistol and the long gun that was beside him. He was still breathing, looking up at me with the most evil eyes. His eyes looked like hot coals in the fire. Next, I went over to the deer hide and removed it from what it was covering and there was my treasure, our daughter Ayita. She was tied up so tight, she couldn't get away. I untied her and hugged her tight. I told her she was safe now. Then I noticed the burn mark on her face, and I wanted him to suffer more before he quit breathing. I dragged him to the fire and placed both of his feet into the fire. I wanted him to feel the pain of the fire before he died. He screamed out in pain, so I knew he was feeling it, then he was dead. Once I knew he was dead, I dragged him away from the fire, so I could sit Ayita closer to get her warm. After I fired the six-signal shots, I sat down with her and just held her tight until the others got to us."

"Marshall McCall and his deputies took the bad man's body and his horse to Linville, which was about ten miles north of where we were. Marshal McCall said he would write the death report and turn the body over to Sheriff Burton for them to arrange the burial. I told him to be sure and bury him face down. Ayita will need help getting her confidence back. This had to be a traumatizing experience for her, so let's keep her out of school next week to let her wound heal, then have her get back into it and try to get things back to normal. We all are very tired. Let's go to bed, tomorrow will be a new day."

Chapter 19

At ten thirty Friday morning, Marshal McCall and his two deputies came riding up to the Adams; house. The marshal told Alan he would stop by on his return from Linville. He had some news to tell Alan about the bad man.

Alan greeted him at the front porch. He asked how Ayita was doing, Alan said, "She's doing pretty well for a little girl that has had such a horrible experience. She was examined by Dr. Hogue and he gave us a special salve for the burn."

The marshal said he needed to tell him more about the bad man.

Alan said to follow him down to the shanty where Sloppy was staying and they would drink some coffee and talk away from Ayita. The two deputies told the marshal they would ride on into town to be with their families, if that was alright. The marshal said, "that's fine, but to go by my office and let Deputy Moore know I will be back there in a little while."

Sloppy was sitting in the shanty drinking coffee and staying warm when Alan knocked on his door. He said, "Come in," and in walks Alan and Marshal McCall. They each pour them a cup of coffee, and the marshal said that the bad man was more of a wanted man than we knew about. He was a Shawnee Indian who went by the name of Tunga. He was wanted for killing a young little Cherokee girl in North Carolina and for molesting a young white girl from north Georgia, but she was able to escape him and he vanished and was never found. The Shawnees expelled him from the tribe for attempting to molest a young Indian girl. There was a five-hundred-dollar reward for his capture dead or alive and I have it for you."

Alan said, "I didn't kill him for any reward, I tracked him, found him and killed him for what he did to my daughter."

Marshal McCall said, "I know, but this money was put up as a reward long before you ever found him. I know you could make good use of it, so take it. You could give it to Ayita to have for her education later or just put it in the bank for her."

Alan said, "That's a good idea, I will take it and divide it five ways. Because of you and your deputies not able to take any of the reward money and I don't want any of it, I will give Ridge and Lucas Bolin a hundred dollars each, I'll give Sloppy and Yano a hundred dollars each then, I'll give a hundred dollars to Ayita to spend any way she wants to."

Marshal McCall said, "That's a great idea. I know all these people didn't help to get money, they helped to get Ayita back home safe and they deserve it for all their hard work."

When dividing out the reward money, Sloppy said, "give my cut to Ayita, I don't need it and think it may help her to recover."

Alan smiled at Sloppy and said, "Okay ole friend, I will do just that. Ayita will now have two hundred dollars, but I will wait until tomorrow to give it to her."

He rode over to the Bolin's place and gave a surprised Ridge and Lucas a hundred dollars each. Ridge and Lucas both said they didn't help expecting any money, but helped to get Ayita home.

Alan said, "I know, but there was a reward for this bad man, and I want y'all to accept your part. It can help you and your family. Tomorrow I will give Yano and Ayita their money that they know nothing about." He explained the best he could how it came to them and told them to do with it what they wished.

Odina felt guilty for not looking after her children more closely that day, Koda felt guilty for losing her tracks when they were playing their game of 'Find Me', and Sloppy felt guilty for not following the bad man when he saw him riding up Three Bears Trail that day. Alan felt guilty for being at work so far from home when it happened.

The next morning sitting around the table after breakfast, Alan had Ayita and Yano remain so he could talk with them. He said, "The bad man that took Ayita was a wanted man from two other parts of the country and there was a reward for him dead or alive. The reward was five hundred dollars. No one in the search party knew anything about a reward, everyone just wanted to help. Marshal McCall learned of it when he arrived in Linville with the body of the bad man. The reward money was given to Marshal McCall to deliver to me. I gave Ridge and Lucus a hundred dollars each for all their help, plus they could really use it. I tried to give Sloppy a hundred dollars, but he said he didn't need it, he said give it to Ayita to buy something she wants. So, Yano, here is a hundred dollars for you for being so much help. Ayita, here is two hundred dollars for you to save or spend on anything you want or need.

Alan looked at his children to see their response." Yano was smiling, this was the most money he had ever seen. Ayita had a puzzled look on her face, because at her young age, she had never had any money. Alan could tell she had something to say and when she spoke up, she asked if this was enough money to buy her and Koda each a horse to ride. Alan was so proud of this daughter of his for her thoughtfulness and bravery. He said, "That is probably more than enough to buy two horses with."

Ayita said, "If there is money left, she would like to give it to the school to help buy supplies that are always needed."

Alan said, "We will go next Thursday or Friday to the livery stable and ask them what they have available or if they know of someone that has horses for sale." He was amazed how his children looked out for one another, especially the twins, Ayita and Koda.

Chapter 20

It's had been three weeks now since and brought Ayita home. She had gone back to school and the burn on her face healed. The scar on her face would probably disappear over time. Alan was able to purchase two horses for ninety dollars with Ayita's reward money and she gave one hundred and ten dollars to her school to buy more supplies. Alan and Odina were so proud of Ayita caring and giving heart. She now has a Philly paint named Bella and Koda has a light brown Colt named Rusty, now all three children could ride their own horse to school.

For the past two weeks, Alan had been catching the train to Rockford to work three days a week. Sloppy was still staying in the shanty which made Alan feel better. Odina and the children are also happy that Sloppy was still there.

Yano had been drawing up plans for the addition to the little cabin at the lake, just as his father had asked him to do. He really wanted to go back to the little cabin and check on the Wolf pups, but he didn't dare ask right now to go alone. Yano didn't know it, but his father wanted to check on the Wolf pups too. Alan knew they had probably left the den by now, and he wanted to find tracks or other signs that they would leave. Yano showed his father the plans for the addition that he had drawn up and the lumber they would need from the sawmill. Alan was impressed with how much thought Yano put into this assignment. Even though they would need to add more as they went along, this would be a good start. He told Yano to carry that order to the sawmill after school and tell Jackson or Larry that he would pay for it when he got back in town. "When it's ready, we'll see if Sloppy will go with you to pick it up in the large wagon and use our mule to pull the wagon."

The following Wednesday after school, Sloppy went with Yano to the sawmill to pick up the lumber. Alan would get home later that night and go back to the sawmill Thursday morning to pay for the lumber.

When Alan went to town Thursday to pay for the lumber, he was approached by Marshall McCall. The marshal told him that the mayor and Township Council had suggested that Shepherd Springs appoint a sheriff to enforce the laws in town.

Alan looked at him with a puzzled look on his face and said, "You are the marshal, why do we need a sheriff?"

The marshal said, "I'm a U.S. Marshal with arrest powers over this territory and my main office is in this town, but my duties sometimes carry me far away from here. This town has grown so much that it needs a local sheriff to enforce the law in this town. Your name was brought up as a very good candidate for the job, if you would consider it."

Alan was very humbled by this consideration, and he would like to be close to home with his job, but he said that he had given his word to Mr. Stockburn to work for two years as his Superintendent over the coal mines in Rockford. "I do appreciate the mayor and council for thinking of me, but I won't go back on my word with Mr. Stockburn and must decline the offer. He's been too good to me." Alan tells the marshal he knows a good honest man that might consider this position, if asked and he only lives one mile out of town. Clyde Bolin is a good man that helped me when we first came here. He's a hard worker and honest too. I'm sure everybody in town knows and respects Clyde Bolin."

Marshal McCall said, "I know Clyde and his name was on the list along with a few others."

Alan said, "I don't know if he would take the job or not, but if he did, he would serve the citizens well."

Friday afternoon when the kids returned from school, Alan told Yano that they would take the wagon load of lumber to the cabin in the morning and would check on the Wolf pups after they unloaded the lumber. He said, "We will leave at daybreak and be back home before dark."

Yano was very excited to go back to the cabin and check on the Wolf pups, but he still wanted to go on an adventure alone again.

Alan asked Sloppy if he wanted to ride out there with them.

Sloppy said he would really enjoy that and that he was thinking of heading back to his place Monday morning to stay a few weeks. He needed to check on some things there.

Chapter 21

With Yano on his horse, Smokie and Alan and Sloppy in the wagon, they arrived at the cabin with a load of lumber.

Once the lumber was unloaded, Alan asked Sloppy if he wanted to go with them to check on the Wolf pups. "No, he said, I'll just stay here, build a fire in the wood stove and lay down for a while."

Alan and Yano left riding double on Smokie and carrying a long rope. They rode to the chair tree's location and looked up at the cave where they had seen the pups. Alan had his telescope with him as he climbed the same tree as before. He watched the entrance for several minutes, but didn't see any movement. He climbed down from the tree and told Yano they would need to walk and climb to the top of the mountain and use the rope to repel down to the cave to get a better look. Yano was excited to do this with his father and a little curious of what they might find or what might find them. When they reached the top, Alan pointed to the rocks he stacked for a marker and said, "The cave is directly under us, we just couldn't see it from here." Alan tied the rope to a tree and threw the long end over the cliff's edge. He explained to Yano how they would use the rope and told him not to let go, even if his feet slipped out from under him, "don't let go of the rope. Rope burns on your hands are a lot better than a busted head on the rocks."

Yano understood.

Alan started down the cliff first and when he reached the narrow ledge, he told Yano to come on and do as he told him.

Yano repelled down like he had done it a hundred times and reached the ledge beside his father. They were standing at the entrance to the cave, getting their eyes focused to see in the darkness. Alan had his forty-four-caliber revolver in his hand as he entered slowly. Yano was right behind him. They didn't hear anything and couldn't tell how far this cave went back into the mountain. Alan was thinking he should have brought a candle for light, but all he had were a few matches in his pocket. They backed out of the cave and Alan spotted a small pine sapling growing in some dirt on a ledge next to him. He cut it down with his knife and scraped the bark off of it. He lit the end to serve as a torch to better see inside the cave. It worked well enough for them to see the back of the cave and that there were no animals in there. They could see the ground well and there were no tracks from the wolves anywhere in that cave. There was no fur, no scat or no bones from any animals that they may have fed on.

Alan and Yano are both confused. They know they saw the pups there, why wasn't there any sign? Were these pups just the Spirits of the Wolf they were seeing? It makes no sense in one way; in another way it makes sense. Alan knew he heard the howling of the Wolf several times and saw the images of the Wolves a few times, but never found any sign of Wolves. However, at every location of the howling of the Wolves, something very special was found. He backed out of the cave again and cut a few more sticks of pine to use as torches and went back in. This time they noticed, on the left wall, a drawing of a Wolf and under it the letters *"Wa Ya"*. This drawing appeared to have been carved in the rock side wall by a sharp object. Having better light in this cave helped. They kept looking and when they inspected the right wall, they could see a ledge like a shelf, on top of the shelf was a pick-ax, an iron staub and a heavy hammer. Under the ledge was a streak embedded in the rock that looked like gold, Alan was pretty sure it was gold, so he took the iron staub that has the flattened end and the hammer, then chiseled out a chunk. They stepped outside the cave again for better light. It was gold embedded in the chunk of rock he chiseled out of the wall. Alan was sure that this was where Fred Smith had been and probably found a lot of gold there. The area was just like the area where he found the gold on his land that he believed Fred hid there. He told Yano they would leave now and check on Sloppy, then head back home. When they come back, they would be better prepared.

Alan was really puzzled about the Wolf pups that he knew he saw there, but no signs of them ever being there. The drawing on the wall of a Wolf with the word *"WaYa'* scratched under the drawing. Wa-Ya was Cherokee for Wolf. He had so many questions. *There was no easy access or exit to the cave, just like the cave he found the buried gold in. Was this Fred Smith's secret place? What about the drawing on the wall that appeared to be done by the Cherokee Indian? Was Fred Smith Cherokee or part Cherokee Indian? Ole Sloppy may have the answers to some of these questions.*

As they climbed up to the to the top using the rope and were walking back down the mountain, Alan told Yano not to say anything about the gold being in that cave or the tools they found. We will just talk about the drawing on the wall and that the pups were gone and no sign of them ever being there.

When they got back to the cabin, they found Sloppy taking a nap on the bunk in the cabin.

Sloppy woke up and said it got so warm in the cabin with the fire in the wood stove, that he fell asleep.

Alan with a laugh said, "It sure is cozy in here, but we need to head on back home now."

Chapter 22

On the slow ride back home, Alan told Sloppy that the Wolf pups were gone, but something was very unusual about the pups he saw.

Sloppy asked what was unusual about them being gone, they always leave their den when reaching a certain age.

Alan said, "Yes, I know that, but they left no sign that they were ever there. There were no tracks, no Wolf hair, no fecal matter or smell, no bones from meals they would have had and absolutely no sign whatsoever in that cave or on the outside of it."

Sloppy said, "That is strange, a wild animal will always leave signs and as good a tracker as you are on tracking, but not finding any signs tells me more about the Spirit of the Wolf. Maybe they were Spirit Pups. That could explain why we never seen any tracks."

Alan said, "We did find something of interest in the cave. A drawing of a Wolf was on the wall and under the drawing was the word *Wa Ya* carved in the wall."

Sloppy spoke up and said something was telling him that Fred Smith was there. "It just sounds like something Fred would do."

Alan said, *"Wa Y"* means wolf in Cherokee. Do you know if Fred was Cherokee?"

Sloppy said, "Fred's mother was Cherokee, and his father was half Cherokee, and their tribal clan was the Wolf Clan."

So much of this was making sense now to Alan. Alan's mother was Cherokee, and her tribal clan was the Wolf Clan. His wife, Odina was Cherokee, and her tribal clan was the Wolf Clan. Alan had heard the howling of the Wolf and so had Odina, Yano, Ayita and Sloppy. Something of importance had always been found at the location of the howling Wolf. Sloppy was the only one that wasn't Indian that had heard the howling of the Wolf. The first time Sloppy heard the Wolf, he found his friend Fred Smith dead at that location. He was killed when a tree fell on him. The second time he heard the Wolf was when he fell from the cliff and broke his leg. He was sure Fred sent the Wolf to have him not give up. Alan remembered the elders telling of treasures that could mean many different things.

They were almost to the house when Sloppy asked Alan, "Remember when you asked Yano where did he get those guns and I spoke up and said they were mine?"

Alan said, "Yes, you felt he needed them for protection while we were searching for Ayita."

Sloppy said, "I really bought them for Yano if you would allow it or either keep them put up until you and Odina felt he was mature enough to have them. It would be my way of showing my appreciation to Yano for all he has done and helped you do for me. I know he is just eleven years old now, but he is more mature than some men I know. If you don't want him to have them right now, just keep them in your house to have for protection."

Alan agreed with Sloppy about Yano being mature for his age, but he would keep the guns in his house for protection and allow Yano to take them when he goes hunting or on another one of his adventures. Yano loves you Sloppy and would never ask for or expect any kind of pay for helping you. He really enjoys learning from you and he will always know that these guns are his and given to him by you. Thank you, my friend."

Yano had made it home ahead of them and put Smokie in the pasture and when his father got there, Yano helped unhook the mule and put it in the pasture also. It was about three hours before dark, supper would be ready in about two hours, so Yano got busy finishing up some of his chores.

Sloppy went to the shanty and made some coffee to drink while he was resting.

Alan checked in with Odina and told her what they found and what they didn't find. He told her that the Wolf pups were gone as he expected they would have been, but he couldn't find any sign that they were ever there.

Odina said, "maybe it was intended that the Spirits of the Wolf left no sign, but appeared as a protector and a locator of treasures in the majestic form."

Alan told Odina another interesting find at the cave was a drawing of a Wolf on the left wall of the cave with *Wa Ya* written under it.

She looked at him and asked, "Why would someone draw a Wolf on the wall and write the Cherokee name for Wolf under it?"

Alan said he didn't know, but that was just another part of the mystery.

Yano made his way to the shanty to talk with Sloppy before supper. He asked Sloppy, "Do you believe in the Spirit of the Wolf?"

Sloppy said, "Yes, I do, do you?"

"Yes," Yano said, "Yes, but I don't understand it because I've heard the howls and seen the Wolf pups, but never found any sign."

Sloppy just laughed and said, "that's why it is the Spirit of the Wolf. If you look up to the sky and see shapes of animals formed in the clouds, do you see tracks on the ground from the animals you see?"

Yano understood what he meant by saying that and said, "No, clouds don't leave tracks on the ground."

Alan was sitting in front of the fireplace enjoying time with Ayita, Koda and Nokomis while Odina was preparing supper. Ayita has had a couple of bad nightmares about her ordeal, but was comforted by her family and has had more good days than bad. She was doing well in school and enjoyed doing her chores at home. Her twin brother, Koda, kept an eye on her all the time, he wanted to be her protector too.

Yano returned to the house and joined them by the fire. He asked his father if he could go on an adventure tomorrow, it would be very close to home and he would be back before dark.

Alan asked, "Where was it you want to go and explore?"

Yano said, "the area where the Ginseng grows on the east side of the mountain behind us. I want to go back to where I found the X mark on the ground that was made by rocks on the west side of the mountain."

Alan said, "that is the place we were going to check out, but never had time. It could be the location that's on my map that has an X mark that I thought could have been where the Ginseng was located. Yes Son, you can go there as long as you dig up some Ginseng, so your mother can make some tea and carry that pistol that Sloppy let you borrow in case a mountain lion, or a bear threatens you. Be sure and look for something out of place for that area where the X mark of rocks is located. There could be something buried under the center of the X or close by. Even though this adventure is close to home, and you won't be camping overnight."

Yano was excited to be allowed to go.

On a cool Sunday morning, Yano quickly got his chores done, had a good breakfast and left the house walking. Excited about his adventure, he carried with him a shovel, a burlap sack, his knife and the forty-five-caliber pistol that he thought belonged to Sloppy. He knew where he was going and had no fear of getting lost. He headed southeast from the house observing all the animal tracks on the ground. He listened to all the different sounds that he could hear mixed in with the wind. Yano hoped to see the ghost deer again and maybe he would see some Wolf tracks. When he reached the top of the mountain, he hadn't seen the ghost deer or any Wolf tracks. Yano went over to the east side to dig some Ginseng first, then he would spend the rest of the day exploring the area where the X mark that he found was. After digging enough Ginseng for his mother, he went over to the steeper west side of the mountain to look for the X mark he had found some time ago. Even though that side was steep with a lot of large rocks, he remembered a section that ran north and south that was like an old trail. He could walk on that section with ease and the area where the X mark was located was on flat ground. There were many rocks on that side of the mountain, and he was having a hard time locating the X mark. He remembered his father telling him to look for something out of place and at the X mark, dig underneath the center of it. Walking north and south on that trail, he was unable to locate the X mark. There were so many rocks on the ground it was hard to see. Yano decided to climb up higher, so he could look down on the trail in hopes of seeing the X mark shape better. He climbed up and got on top of a large boulder and sat there enjoying the peaceful feeling that he got when alone and exploring. He looked down on the trail to the north, then to the south and spotted the X mark to his south. When he was at ground level with it, he couldn't see it as plain as when he was above it looking down. He was all excited as he climbed down to the X mark. He studied his surroundings for anything that looked out of place. While he was standing on the X, he noticed the rocks beside him about three feet up with one flat rock lying against the steep part of the mountain. It looked like a door. It was a flat-looking rock about one foot wide and two foot long with another flat rock sticking out like a roof over this little door. To him, this looked out of place, but first he dug under the X mark. He found nothing there, so he put everything back like it was. Still concentrating on that rock that looked like a little door with a roof over it, he began to try and remove it to see what was behind it. He took the shovel and scraped away the dirt on both sides of the rock and could tell that it was about four inches thick and wedged in there pretty well. This rock that was wedged in there was very heavy for an eleven-year-old and he knew if there was a hidden treasure behind this rock, he would want to put it back to look natural. Yano decided he would try to remove the rock and worry about putting it back later. He was able to get his fingers to the back of this rock and pull it forward a little. He had to dig more at the bottom of the rock. He braced himself and was able to pull this heavy rock out and it fell about three feet, just missing his foot. Behind the rock was a hole like a small cave. Inside the hole, he could plainly see a wooden box that looked to be about one foot square in size. Yano was overcome with excitement. The wooden box was very heavy as he tried to pull it out of the hole. He was finally able to get the box out and set it on the level ground. Nervous and excited, he removed the lid to the box.

The first thing he saw inside the box was a piece of folded paper on top and what looked like several cloth tobacco pouches that were full of something. He unfolded the paper and read what was written. In the upper right-hand corner was the date of *October 15, 1845.* Next it read---- *If you found this box, know that it belongs to Fred Smith and if I am still alive, it is still mine. If I have already passed away, then this box and all that it contains belongs to the person that found a map I had hidden with its location marked with an X mark on it.* There was more writing, but Yano wanted to open the tobacco pouches. He opened one at a time to find them full of gold nuggets. He counted fifteen tobacco pouches in the box with every one of them full of gold nuggets. Yano knew he could not carry all of this weight back home and he remembered what his father and Sloppy told him about being secretive about certain treasures he found. He would tell his father and show him the note, but he needed to put all of the gold back in the box and hide it back in the hole. The easiest way to do that, because of the total weight, would be to put the empty box in the hole, then place each pouch in the box and place the lid back on the top. That part was easy, now he needed to get that rock back up there to block the hole and it was heavy. He struggled with the rock, and managed to get it put back in place. He took smaller rocks and filled the gaps and now it looked natural again. He was excited to tell his father and show him the note.

Yano grabbed the bag of Ginseng roots, his shovel and headed home with a big smile on his face. This adventure had been one of his shortest, but the most exciting because he of how he found this treasure alone by looking for something out of place like he was told by his father and by Sloppy.

When Yano walked up to the back door of their house he was greeted by his mother at the back door. She took the bag from him, looked inside and says, "Thank you Yano, now I can make Ginseng tea when we want it."

He smiled and asked where his father was.

She said he was down at the barn.

Yano went to the barn and showed his father the note.

Alan started reading the note and read the last part that Yano didn't read. "It was written that *all the gold did not come from my land, but I found a large vein of gold on government land north of mine.* The last sentence said, *I Fred Smith, upon my death, leave all this gold in this wooden box to the holder of the map with the X mark on it.*"

Signed Fred Smith, October 15, 1845.

Alan asked Yano how much gold was in the box.

Yano said, "It had fifteen tobacco pouches, each one was full of gold nuggets. It was very heavy, and he couldn't bring it home, so he hid it back where it was."

Alan told him he did good and that he was proud of him. "Don't talk about this to anyone. I will tell your mother, but nobody else should know. What you have found will help this family for years Yano and I am so proud of you."

After supper, Alan told Odina of Yano's find. He told her that they would keep it hid where he found it until he could go with Yano and determine how much gold was there. He told her Fred Smith left a note with the box of gold too and that he thought Fred found a rich vein of gold on the north end of their new property.

Sloppy was leaving in the morning and Alan was going to Rockford for three days to work, so he sat with Sloppy a while before going to bed. He told Sloppy that he wished he would just stay here, but he understood how he loved mountain life.

Sloppy said, "I will stay two or three weeks at my place, then don't be surprised if you see smoke coming out of the flu at the shanty."

Alan said, "Well don't be surprised, if we don't see or hear from you within three weeks, that me and Yano come riding up to your place."

Sloppy laughed and said, "I'll be back, but whenever I die, do me a favor and bury me on the right side of my cabin on that little rise where it's flat."

Chapter 23

It's the spring of 1861. Alan was still making his trips to Rockford and working three days a week.

Sloppy had been showing back up at the Adam's place every two or three weeks and staying a few weeks.

Yano was now twelve years old and had grown taller. He still loved going on adventures.

Ayita's scar on her face was almost invisible and she was doing well in school. Her twin brother, Koda, was doing well in school, also, and was keeping a watchful eye on her. Nokomis was still being home-schooled by her mother. They had finished the addition of the cabin at the lake at the north end of their property. The family had already spent a few weekends there enjoying the lake and panning for gold. Abraham Lincoln was the 16th President of the United States. A civil war began in April between the Union and the Confederacy.

Clyde Bolin turned down the appointment of sheriff and recommended his son, Ridge, for the job after he spoke in favor of the job. Ridge Bolin, at twenty-six years old was appointed the first Sheriff of Shepherd Springs, Virginia in November of 1860.

Alan cashed in some of the gold that Yano found and purchased twenty head of cattle. In an agreement with Clyde Bolin, they put them on his land where there was more grazing land. They would share in the duties and profit when they took them to sell. Lucus Bolin, Yano and Koda Adams would care for them and move them from pasture to pasture when needed.

It had been a month since Sloppy had come out of the mountains and Alan was worried. In two days, Alan had to catch the train to Rockford to take care of some important mining business and couldn't go check on him until he got back.

Yano said, "I can go. I know the way and I'm worried about Sloppy too."

Alan felt confident that Yano could handle this chore as well as any man, so he approved. He gave Yano instructions and told him to load supplies on PoGo instead of the mule, so he could make better time. "If Sloppy is okay, and just wants to stay, give him the supplies he needs. You can spend the night there to rest and help him, then head back as soon as you can. If you are not back by Wednesday night, I will leave early Thursday morning to come and check on you and Sloppy. He seemed to be doing so well last time he was here and when he left to go back, I'm thinking something must have happened for him to be over a week late coming by here."

They all knew how much Sloppy loved mountain life, but they also knew his health was not as good as it once was and that's the reason he would come out of the mountains every two or three weeks. It had been over four weeks now and that wasn't not like him unless something was wrong.

Yano was loaded up and heading out at noon on Friday. He rode his horse, Smokie, and led his mother's horse, PoGo, that was loaded with some supplies. He should make good time and would probably stop and rest a few hours hoping to arrive at Sloppy's place by tomorrow afternoon. Yano was more scared than excited about this adventure. As grown as he thought he was, he wasn't sure if he was mature enough to handle what he might find when he got there. He could see well enough to ride in the dark and made it to the stacked rocks where he knew to go to the right. Yano rode about another hour, but it was darker down in the valley, so he stopped to give the horses a break and rest a few hours before continuing on further. He built a fire and laid his bed roll out. Laying there, he could see the stars above and hear the sounds of the Appalachian Mountains and he knew he was in his element, at this moment, but he couldn't help worrying what he might find. All the instructions he received from Sloppy about what to do when he died was on his mind. Sloppy said he wanted to be buried on his land. He would always remember Sloppy telling him that when he died to go to the chair tree where you retrieved my rope and hat for me, then go to the top of the ridge, staying in line with the chair tree, repel down to a ledge, then look for something out of place there. Yano knew that it would be a treasure, that he looked for there, but he was not ready for that. He and Sloppy had created a bond of friendship and Yano wanted it to continue. He fell asleep, but was awakened about one hour later by the eerie screams of a Bobcat. The horses were nervous, so he got up to calm them. Yano was frightened at first by the Bobcat scream, but was okay a few seconds later when he knew it wasn't a mountain lion. Yano loaded back up and continued on his journey in the dark. He hoped Sloppy was fine and just didn't want to leave his place yet. He remembered Sloppy saying that Spring was his favorite season and maybe he was just enjoying the warmer weather and the new greenery coming alive in the forest.

By traveling so much at night, Yano had saved half a day of traveling and it was a little after the noon hour. He could see the chair tree up ahead and he knew he was only a half mile from Sloppy's cabin. As he approached the chair tree that was on the left side of the trail, he noticed a large hole on the right that looked like it had been freshly dug. At first, he thought that was where Sloppy had been digging for gold. Then, he could see Sloppy's horse, Topper, lying dead just above where the hole was. Yano got off his horse and walked over to Topper, he couldn't tell how he died. Yano called out for Sloppy, but got no answer.

Chapter 24

Back at the Adams' house, Alan was now worried about two people and thinking he should have gone with Yano. The Stockburn Mining Company had plans to open another section of the mine up and as the Superintendent, Alan had to be there. When he got home Wednesday night, he would load up and go to Sloppy's cabin if Yano was not home by then.

~~~~~~

Yano slowly approached Sloppy's cabin and noticed a human figure at the coral. He didn't call Sloppy's name because he couldn't tell if it was him. The man at the coral heard Yano riding up the trail. He took cover from this intruder until he recognized the lead horse as Smokie, then he saw Yano. Yano recognized Sloppy at the same time and called out his name.

Sloppy yelled back, "Yano!"

Yano smiled and was feeling proud of himself for finding Sloppy's place after only being there once before, but what he was the happiest about was that Sloppy was standing there, not injured and not looking sick. Yano
~~~~~~

rode up to the coral and said, "You're late, and we have been worried about you. Father had to go to Rockford, so he approved for me to come here and check on you."

Sloppy said, "Well that shows he has a lot of confidence in you as I do, but I am alright. Ole Topper died on me, so I have been digging a hole to bury him. Digging a hole is a lot harder than it used to be and I have more digging to do for it to be big enough."

Yano said he was sorry about Topper. "I can help with the digging while we still have plenty of daylight."

Sloppy said, "I can use the help, thanks. We will have to take my mule and rope, so we can drag Topper to his grave."

They removed the supplies from PoGo, so Yano could ride him bareback and Sloppy would ride Smokie with his saddle down to the grave digging spot. When they got there, Yano jumped in the hole with a pick and shovel and started to work. Sloppy told him to dig it a little longer by using the pick and he would use the shovel to shovel out the dirt. After they had been digging for an hour, Sloppy said, "That's good enough, let's drag him to the hole and start covering him up." Sloppy was sad to have lost his loyal friend of eighteen years. Once that was completed and the grave was covered with rocks, Sloppy sat on the ground resting. He told Yano, that when he died, he wanted to be buried on that little rise on the right side of his cabin," then he asked Yano if he would see that his wishes were honored.

Yano said, "Yes Sir," but he hoped it would be a long time now.

They rode back up to the cabin after completing the burial to rest and cook up something to eat. Yano told Sloppy he could go back with him in the morning and stay with them for a while, if he wanted to. He said, "My father and mother would be happy to see you riding up with me to stay in the shanty again."

Sloppy laughed a little with sadness and said he did need to go back to get another horse and pick up some more supplies.

Yano said he would go out and take care of the horses and the mule; he brought some grain for them.

Sloppy said he would start cooking up some grub. He had caught a couple trout earlier to have for supper tonight and he could eat one and Yano could have one. "I'll fry up some corn fritters to."

Sounded good to Yano. Both were very tired, so after supper, they talked a little, then went to sleep. Yano was sad that Topper had died, but happy to see that Sloppy was doing alright and he agreed to go back with him.

When morning came, they saddled up Smokie and put Sloppy's saddle on PoGo and got started on the long ride home, taking Sloppy's mule with them. Riding by the chair tree, Sloppy stopped and told Yano to look up to the top of the mountain on their right. He said, "That's where you retrieved my rope and hat."

Yano said, "Yes, I remember."

Then Sloppy pointed up to the top and asked, "so you see that large boulder up there about twenty feet from the top that looks like it has a dark hole under it?"

Yano said, "Yes Sir, I see it."

"Well, that's where you will need to look for something out of place like I told you."

Yano listened and took all that in, but hoped it would be a long time before he had to do that.

They had rode over halfway home when they stopped and made camp. Yano could have ridden on more, but he knew Sloppy was tired and needed to rest. This adventure of Yano's was all about finding Sloppy's place again and finding him alive. Alan had told Yano, "If Sloppy is alive, see if he will ride back with you to stay with us a while. If Sloppy wants to stay at his place, leave him the supplies you carried there, then you head home the next morning."

Chapter 25

It was about four o'clock Monday afternoon when Yano and Sloppy rode up to the front porch of the Adam's house.

Odina was standing on the front porch with a smile on her face, because her oldest son was home, and he had Sloppy with him. She noticed that Sloppy was riding PoGo, not his horse Topper. She told Sloppy, "we've been worried about you because you are about two weeks late on coming out of the mountains."

"I apologize," he said, "but ole Topper wasn't feeling well enough to make the trip, then he died. I had been digging his grave for two days and would still be digging if Yano hadn't shown up and helped me."

Odina told Yano to put the horses and mule in the pasture and for Sloppy to get settled in the shanty. She advised that she would have supper ready in two hours. Yano and Sloppy both were hungry and ready to have some of Odina's cooking.

Sloppy took his saddle bags and other gear and secured it in the shanty. Inside one of the saddle bags was a pouch full of gold that he planned on using to purchase another horse from Jacob Jenkins at the Livery Stable.

Sitting at the supper table, Odina told Yano he would need to go to school tomorrow with Koda and Ayita. She didn't want him getting behind with his education.

He would rather stay home and talk more with Sloppy about the Spirit of the Wolf and to plan his next adventure, but he would do as his mother said and talk with Sloppy when he got home.

Monday night, sixty miles northeast of Shepherd Springs, in Rockford, Virginia, Alan couldn't help but be concerned about what Yano found or if he was even able to find Sloppy's place at all. Alan wouldn't know anything until he got home Wednesday night. Alan was the Superintendent over this new coal mining operation and had to oversee all of its operations. He had been very busy, but still worried about his son and friend.

When Tuesday morning came, all of the children were up doing their chores, then after breakfast, Yano, Ayita and Koda were off to school.

Sloppy told Odina he needed to go to town and try to buy a horse from Jacob Jenkins at the Livery Stable and asked if he could borrow PoGo.

Odina said, "You can borrow my horse, but I need to go to town, also. We could just hook up the buckboard and me and Nokomis could ride with you. I would like to send a telegram to Alan in Rockford to let him know you and Yano are back and doing well. You know he is plenty worried about y'all and if he could get the message, he wouldn't have to worry so much."

Sloppy said, "That's a good idea, I will put my saddle in the buckboard, and we can pick up any supplies you may need while we are there. I will need to go see Beanstalk first though." Sloppy had about one pound of gold to sell to Beanstalk and if he bought it, it should be more than enough to purchase a horse and all the supplies they need.

When they arrived in town, Sloppy went to the Trading Post while Odina and Nokomis walked to the telegraph office. Odina asked Wilbur Williams if he could send a telegram to her husband Alan in Rockford.

Wilbur looked at Odina and asked if this was more bad news?

Odina said, """no, good news this time," and advised him what to send. She said, he won't be back to the hotel until tonight, so they could leave the message at the desk for him." The fee for sending the telegraph was twenty-five cents.

Beanstalk purchased seventeen ounces of gold from Sloppy, paying him three hundred and six dollars.

Odina and Nokomis met back up with Sloppy and went with him to the Livery Stable.

Sloppy asked Jacob if he had any good horses for sale.

Jacob said, "Yes, he had several good horses in the coral around back." When they went to look at them, little Nokomis ran ahead of them and stood at the fence looking at them.

Sloppy spied one he was interested in, but he kept watching Nokomis. She was watching a little filly that was dark brown with a white star on her forehead. He asked her if she liked that filly.

Nokomis smiled and said, "No, I love her."

Sloppy just smiled and called Jacob off to the side to tell him what he wanted and asked the price. Sloppy paid Jacob the amount he wanted and said they would be back after they picked up some supplies at the General Store.

When they got to the General Store, he told Odina to get what she needed, and he would pay for it.

She looked at him as if to say, "no you are not going to pay for my supplies," but he spoke first and said, "Alan can settle up with me when he gets home."

She was fine with that. With all their supplies loaded in the buckboard, they went back to the Livery Stable. Sloppy removed his saddle from the buckboard and told Odina he would be back after a while for them to go on. He wanted to go to Roosters Tavern for a drink.

Jacob told Sloppy the four-year-old gelding he bought was good on the trails and was very calm, but the two-year-old filly he purchased was a good horse to ride, but had a little spunk sometimes. Jacob said the filly had no name, but the chestnut-colored gelding was called Chester. Sloppy put his saddle on the filly to ride and he would lead Chester. He had a plan of what to say when he got back to the Adams' house.

After Sloppy had his drink at Rooster', he got back on Three Bears Trail and headed back to the shanty that he was staying in at the Adams' place. As he was riding past the Bolin's path to their place, he heard horses coming up behind him. When he looked back, he saw Yano, Ayita and Koda riding up faster than he was going. Yano could tell it was Sloppy that was in front of them, but he didn't know why he had two horses. When they caught up with him, everybody was all smiles when Yano asked him why he had two horses.

Sloppy said with a laugh, "one is for riding, and one is for hauling supplies."

Yano knew that wasn't true because Sloppy had the mule for hauling supplies, but he didn't question him anymore.

Sloppy told them to ride on home and help their mother unload the supplies from the buckboard, he would be there soon. As Sloppy started up the path to the shanty and barn, he could see the buckboard had been unloaded and PoGo put in the pasture. He also noticed Nokomis walking his way from the house with Odina right behind her. He got to the barn, he removed the saddle from the filly, then put Chester and the filly in the pasture.

Nokomis hopped up on the rail of the fence and said, "You bought my favorite horse."

Odina standing behind Nokomis, but looking at Sloppy like, "what have you done now?"

Sloppy said, "Yes, I bought two horses. One for riding and one for hauling, but I don't think I like the filly, she's a little spunky and a little small for me." Then he said, "Nokomis, she has no name, so if you name her, she can be yours, if it's alright with your mother and father."

Odina walked over to Sloppy and told him, "You can't do that. You need the money you spent on her and we cannot accept her."

Sloppy told Odina, "I have no family, y'all have taken me in and always looked after me and treated me like family." Then he said, "I don't tell everybody this, but I have plenty of money. I have been fortunate to find more gold than I will ever need for just me. I don't want much and it doesn't take much for me to survive. I saw the way her eyes lit up when she saw this filly at the

Livery Stable and just knew she had to have it. So please, talk to Alan and the both of you allow her to have this filly. I rode her all the way back and she is safe and easy to control."

Odina hugged Sloppy and told him he was family.

Nokomis came running, yelling out loud, "Morning Star, Morning Star is her name. Can she be my horse Mother?"

Odina said, "If your father approves tomorrow night when he gets home, she can." Odina knew how to explain it to Alan, so he couldn't say no. Yano, Ayita and Koda came to the barn and saw Nokomis all excited when she told them that the filly's name was Morning Star and if Father approved, she would be hers.

Yano thought he already knew that by the way Sloppy laughed and told them why he bought two horses. Yano, Ayita and Koda started explaining to Nokomis how to care for the filly in case she became hers.

There were a few more hours of light, so Sloppy saddled up Chester to see how he rode. He said he was going to the fishing hole at the waterfall and back. Chester was a big muscular horse with a calm personality, and tomorrow he wanted to try him out pulling the buckboard.

Chapter 26

At eight thirty Wednesday night, Alan arrived in Shepherd Springs. His train ride from Rockford was better because of the telegraph message he received the night before. The message stated that his son and best friend were home and doing well. There was a livestock car on this train for passengers to carry their horses with them. Alan carried his horse, Scout, with him when he traveled to Rockford for work. When Scout was unloaded from the train, Alan rode his three miles home. He could see smoke coming from the flu at the shanty and a light from the inside. He stopped there, first, to speak to Sloppy and see with his own eyes that he was alright. Alan was so happy to see that his friend was well, had no broken bones or sickness. He didn't stay, but a minute. He said, "we will talk later ole friend, you just rest and get a good night's sleep and I'm going to see the rest of my family now."

He didn't ask Sloppy why he was so late coming out of the mountains, so he would hear it from Yano first.

Odina and Yano were still up, waiting for Alan. The other children were in bed. Alan was greeted at the front door by Odina. She had a bowl of bean soup and corn fritters ready for him because she knew he would be hungry.

Yano told his father that, "Topper had died and Sloppy was having a hard time digging the grave big enough, so I helped him with the digging, then we buried Topper close to the chair tree. I carried supplies for him and found him okay. He said he would come with me, so he could buy another horse. Yano said he made good time going there because he traveled more at night than they did the time before. It was slow coming back though because we brought his mule with us."

Alan looked at Odina, they were both smiling and thinking the same thing. He told Yano that they were so proud of him for taking on this adventure on his own without complaint. He said, "You are on the right road to manhood and those were some very important miles you traveled."

Yano was happy that his parents were proud of him, and he felt sure they would allow him to take another adventure. He went to bed while Alan and Odina sat in the rocking chairs in front of the fireplace.

Alan was drinking coffee and enjoying the feeling of being home. Odina told him, "Tuesday morning; we went to town with Sloppy, so I could send the telegram to you and Sloppy could see about purchasing a horse from Jacob. Sloppy went to the Trading Post where he sold some gold to Beanstalk while Nokomis and I sent the telegram. Then all three of us went to the Livery Stable to look at horses. Sloppy saw one he liked, and so did Nokomis," she said with a laugh. "Then Sloppy stepped over to Jacob discussing price, I guess, while Nokomis stayed on the rail of the fence admiring the little filly. Next, we all left the stables to go to the General Store to get supplies. Sloppy left his new horse there until we got all the supplies we needed loaded up in the buckboard. Sloppy paid for all the supplies, but I told him not to do that, he didn't need to pay for our supplies. He said he would settle up with you when you got home, so tell him you need to pay him for the supplies we got."

Alan said he would tomorrow.

"I then carried him back to the stables, so he could get the horse he bought and ride it back. He told us to go home, he was going to Roosters to have a drink, then he would be home. The kids got home from school before Sloppy did and helped unload the supplies and put PoGo back in the pasture. Sloppy rode up a few minutes later and we could see from the house that he had two horses. Nokomis recognized one of the horses as the one she fell in love with at the stable. She ran down to the barn to get a better look. We all followed and heard Sloppy say he bought two, one for riding and one for hauling his supplies, but he didn't want that filly, she was a little small for him and she had some spunk to her." Odina said, "Then he asked Nokomis if she liked that filly."

Nokomis said, "no, she loved her."

"Sloppy told Nokomis if she would name her, she could have her as her own horse, if your mother and father approved. I told Sloppy he didn't need to spend his money; he would need it to live on. Sloppy said, 'well I have plenty of money, more than enough actually, but what I don't have is family, y'all are my family, so let me do this for Nokomis.' I saw the way she looked at that filly when we were at the stables, and I knew she had to have it. Nokomis came running to us saying "Morning Star" is her name, it's Morning Star because she has a star on her forehead. Sloppy told me to ask you to allow her to have it."

Alan said he couldn't say no to that and Sloppy was family. "I'll thank him tomorrow when I pay him for the supplies."

As Alan and Odina were going to bed, he looked in on Ayita, Koda and Nokomis that were sound asleep. Yano was in bed in the loft still awake and planning his next adventure. He was thinking of going back to the cabin at the lake. There was so much more to explore there, but more important, he was hoping to see the Wolves again. He had no explanation why they left no tracks, but he does know he and his father saw them. He could feel their spirit and had no fear of the Wolf. Yano felt like the Wolves would allow him to see them again if he was alone and believed in their spirit.

Thursday morning, all the children were up, finished their chores and had breakfast and Yano, Ayita and Koda were off to school.

Sloppy didn't come to breakfast and had just got up to make coffee. Alan would carry him a couple of biscuits and ham when he walked down to the shanty to talk and have coffee with him.

Alan asked Sloppy, "how much do I owe you for the supplies you purchased."

Sloppy laughed and said, "I don't know what you're talking about."

Alan already knew that Sloppy wasn't going to let him pay, so he would have to think of some other way to make it right. Alan knew this was Sloppy's way of helping them like they had helped him.

Nokomis and her mother were walking down to the barn to see Morning Star. Nokomis really wanted to ride her. Odina thought that was a good idea, so she put a bridle on Morning Star and a bridle on PoGo so she could ride with her. They would ride them bareback. Odina helped her daughter get on the filly, then they both rode by the shanty where Alan and Sloppy were standing on the porch watching. Nokomis had a big smile on her face as she waved to her father and Sloppy and in a loud voice said, "I love her!"

Sloppy looked at Alan and said, "that's the best money I ever spent and don't you try to take my joy away."

Alan said, "No Sir, I won't."

Nokomis was riding that filly bareback like someone that had been riding for years. She looked so natural sitting on Morning Star. They got on Three Bears Trail and went south toward town.

Alan thought they might be going to the Bolins two miles away to show them Morning Star. When they came back about an hour later, Alan and Sloppy were down at the barn. Sloppy was showing Alan the horse he bought.

Odina said they rode to the Bolins to show them Morning Star and they were very happy for Nokomis. Odina told Alan and Sloppy that Nokomis did very well and smiled the whole time riding her. Odina walked over to Sloppy, hugged him and said, "Thank you for making our little girl so happy."

This made Sloppy feel good and he truly feels like family.

When the children got home from school today, Yano told his parents that the teacher said there would be no school next Thursday and Friday, she had to go out of town on some family business, but would be back the following Monday. Yano started planning his next adventure and would talk to his parents tonight and ask for their approval because he knew he could not go when his father was out of town working, he would wait and leave next Thursday morning, if they approved.

Yano asked for permission and approval to go on another adventure, he promised to do all his chores before leaving and finish up on the chores when he returned. He told them he wanted to go to the cabin at the lake again and would close himself up in the cabin in the dark hours. He felt the Spirit of the Wolf was wanting him to see them again. He would look for signs of the Wolf while doing his exploring. He said he wouldn't climb any cliffs and would be safe. He would like to leave next Thursday morning and come back Saturday, so he could do his chores on Sunday. Yano said he would carry food supplies with him, but, also, would catch fish to eat. He had it all planned out and would appreciate their approval.

Odina and Alan told Yano to let them sleep on it and they would have an answer when he got home from school tomorrow.

Yano was pretty confident that they would let him go so he continued on with his plans. When he got home Friday, his parents told him he could go on this adventure next Thursday through Saturday, but he was to be home by noon on Saturday. Yano wanted to know if he could carry the two firearms that Sloppy let them borrow.

Alan spoke up and said, "Sloppy bought that rifle and pistol for you to have whenever we thought you were ready. We both feel you are responsible enough to have them now. You need to thank Sloppy for this generous gift."

Yano went directly to see Sloppy and thanked him for the two gifts, then, for the next two days he got busy with his chores. After lunch Saturday, all the children rode their own horses bareback to help Nokomis get used to riding her new filly. Their parents wanted them to be knowledgeable on riding bareback and with a saddle. When they returned, Odina called Yano to the kitchen to show him how to make a meal out of potatoes, onions and ham. She knew that he could carry those items with him and cook his own meal.

Chapter 27

Yano was excited that Thursday morning had come, and he was ready to start his adventure. His mother had given him a cloth bag with enough food items in it to feed him for three days. Yano knew how to hunt, trap and fish for food, but he wouldn't have to. Now he could focus more on exploring.

Alan and Odina understood his love for exploring, he got that desire from them.

Yano approached the cabin slowly, looking for any signs of danger. It was a beautiful day with blue skies and comfortable temperatures. There was no sign of bears at the cabin, where they had broken in searching for food. His first order of business was to unload the supplies and store them in the cabin and make sure he had enough wood for the wood stove to cook on and heat with in the mornings. His father let him bring the small telescope, so he rode down to the chair tree where the cave was. He knew he probably wouldn't see the Wolves there again, but he had to try. Yano climbed the same tree his father had to get a better look at the entrance to the cave. He scoped up and down the side of the mountain for about fifteen minutes, but saw nothing. He rode Smokie further southwest to get on the north side of the mountain where the cave was. He wanted to explore that section of land that he had not seen before. Yano could sense that he was being watched. The trees were full of a new growth of leaves and the ground was covered with bushes and wildflowers making it difficult to see any wildlife. He was not feeling danger from being watched, but protection from danger. Yano was sure it was the Spirit of the Wolf keeping watch over him, but he would sure love to see it. He remained alert for anything of danger to him. He left that area and rode east to look at the land on the east side of the trail to the cabin. He was excited to explore that land he had not seen before. Yano found another cave among some large boulders that was at the bottom of a mountain of large rocks. He wanted to explore it, but remembered what his father told him, he said if you get injured, remember that you are alone. Yano would remember this location and wait until his father could be with him to explore the cave together. This made Yano happy to see places he had never seen before and he usually found something of interest in every acre he explored.

Yano returned to the cabin, removed the saddle from Smokie and gave him feed and water in the coral. When he inventoried his food bag, he found potatoes, one onion, two ham steaks, a slab of bacon, several pieces of flatbread, four biscuits, six eggs and a pouch of beef jerky. After seeing all the food, he would have more time to explore and not have to hunt, trap or fish for his food. He would fry potatoes and onions for supper tonight with ham and flatbread. Tomorrow, he would explore the other side of the lake. He had never been over there before. Their property line on the north end was probably close to the other side of the lake.

When morning came, Yano built a fire in the wood stove to knock the early morning chill off and to cook his breakfast consisting of three eggs, bacon and one biscuit. He checked on Smokie and gave him some sweet feed, then he sat on the porch of the cabin eating and listening to the mountains come alive. He wanted to walk to where he would be exploring today. Yano put some deer jerky and flatbread in his pocket, a canteen full of water and a leather pouch with black powder and forty-five caliber mini balls in it for his muzzle loader rifle around his neck. Also, he would have his forty-five-caliber pistol and his knife on a belt around his waist. Holding his rifle, he started walking to the west end of the lake. The forest was full of green foliage and different colors of wildflowers. The look was totally different from the wintertime look. When he got to the other side of the lake, there were large boulders everywhere he looked. The land was fairly flat for about one hundred yards across to the next small mountain. The sun was peaking over the mountain to the east, and it feltg good to him. Yano climbed up on one of the large boulders to sit, look, listen and think. Like his father, his best thinking was sitting on the porch, Yano got his best thinking done while sitting on a large rock, especially with the sun shining down on him. He sat on top of that rock as though he was hunting, but he wasn't hunting to have food, he was hunting with his eyes to see what he could see. He only carried the rifle and pistol for protection against any wildlife that would try and do him harm. He spotted movement one hundred yards away on the side of the mountain in front of him and took a look through his father's telescope. It was four deer going east, but the ghost deer was not with them. Yano spotted another large boulder in front of him that was a little higher. so he went to it, so he could see better. The top of the rock had a flat surface larger than the other one. There was a large rock on top of that boulder that made the perfect back rest, and Yano used it as such. He took a piece of jerky out of his pocket for a snack, as he used the telescope to scan the side of the mountain in front of him. There was a Red Tail Hawk high above him being chased by Crows. He watched as the Hawk flew higher and higher to get away from the Crows. He was amazed at the bravery of the Crows to attack the mighty Hawk; they couldn't fly as high. Yano spotted more movement to his left on the lower west end of the mountain. Looking through the telescope, it was a squirrel, jumping tree to tree as if it was frightened. Yano then lowered the telescope down to the boulders at the bottom of the mountain where he noticed more movement. He shifted his body to the left, propped his elbows on his knees and tried to focus the telescope on the movement he noticed with his naked eye. He had a good clear view and couldn't believe what he was seeing. Going west were four Wolves. These looked to be half grown Wolves and he thought they were the same four pups that he and his father saw just a few months ago. As he tried to hold the telescope steady, in all his excitement, one of the Wolves stopped moving and turned to face his direction. Yano was over a hundred yards away from these Wolves, but it appeared that this one noticed his movement. He was trying to hold the telescope still, so he could look at them as long as he could. when the other three came and stood next to the first one and now all four were staring in his direction. Yano thought to himself, *these were some amazing animals to notice him so far away.* They stood there staring like they were frozen in time in what seemed like thirty minutes or more. Somehow, Yano knew he would see a Wolf on this trip. It was as if their spirit was calling him to come to this place. Yano's elbow slipped off his knee causing him to lose them with the telescope and when he put it back at their location, they were gone. He searched all over that area with the telescope and could not find them again. Yano was upset, he could have looked at those Wolves all day. Not giving up just yet, he kept searching. They might be sneaking their way over to him. He kept watching and listening.

Yano felt what seemed like a warm breath on the right side of his neck. He slowly turned his body to the right and was nose to nose with a Wolf twice as big as he was. They just stared into each other's eyes, looking into each other's soul. Yano and the Wolf were calm, and not frightened at all. The Wolf lowered his head into Yano's chest and Yano put his hands on each side of the Wolf's head and in a low calm voice said, "Wa Ya," then placed his forehead on the Wolf's forehead. He had touched the Wolf and looked into its soul. Yano was amazed at the size of that Wolf and thought he was the father to the four he just saw. He wanted to hold his head longer, but the Wolf raised his head and stared at Yano. Yano then lowered his head, closed his eyes and spoke to the Wolf saying, "I mean you no harm, I will protect you." When Yano raised his head and opened his eyes, the Wolf was gone. He looked all around, but the Wolf had vanished. Yano sat there in silence wondering if he was dreaming what had just happened or is that how it is with The

Spirit of the Wolf. This meant more to Yano than finding gold, but he didn't understand how they just disappear.

He decided to look for their tracks, he knew where the four were walking and standing. And the big one he touched was there with him, so there should be tracks on the ground close by. Yano got down from the rock and started looking for tracks of the big Wolf. He found his own tracks, but no Wolf tracks were found. Next, he walked across the flat area to the mountain where he saw the deer. He found the tracks of four deer right where he saw them. Then he walked west to where he saw the four Wolves. He knew exactly where it was. He searched for an hour, but no tracks were there either. *How could that be? He saw the four deer and found their tracks. He could see his own tracks. He saw five Wolves, even touched one of them, but they left no tracks.*

Yano headed back to the cabin before it got dark, only this time he would go around the northeast end of the lake. There was so much land there he had yet to explore. He would decide what he would fix for supper when he got back to the cabin, but first, he had to go over one more mountain to see what was on the other side. He would need to go back home tomorrow and even though he hated to leave, he was excited to tell his parents and Sloppy what he saw. He hoped they could explain to him why he could see the Wolves and touch one Wolf, but couldn't find any sign of them being there.

This had been such a mystical adventure for Yano and to gain a tremendous bond with the Spirit of the Wolf made him happy. When he got back to the cabin, he checked on Smokie and then started cooking up his supper. He was having more fried potatoes and onions with a ham steak. After he ate, he just sat on the porch of the cabin and played back in his mind what he had seen today. He could still feel the breath of the Wolf on his neck, how the Wolf put his head on his chest and how they looked into each other's souls. There was an Owl hooting up on the mountain side, and that was a beautiful sound to Yano. He closed himself up in the cabin and tried to go to sleep, but he was too excited to sleep, still thinking about his day. After about an hour, he finally fell asleep and dreamed that the Wolf was in the cabin with him, asleep on the floor next to his bunk. When Yano woke up at daylight, he looked down to the floor, but there was no Wolf there. After breakfast, he washed up what few dishes he used, loaded the food supplies that he had left, put the saddle on Smokie and headed home. He was excited to tell of his experience and hoped his parents would have some answers for him as to why he could see and touch the Wolves, but couldn't find any of their tracks.

Chapter 28

Riding slowly on the trail going home, Yano decided to get a little more exploring done on his way. He turned west to ride between some small mountains to see land he had not seen yet. Yano was amazed at all the large boulders on that land, he couldn't help, but wonder where they came from. He saw the beauty in all of them and how they all were different shapes. Yano knew by going west, he would eventually run into Three Bears Trail and go the rest of the way home. He spotted an animal running across the forest floor that looked like a squirrel, except it was twice as big as the squirrels he had seen and hunted, and the animal's fur was red in color. Yano stopped and used the telescope to get a better look when the animal went up a tree. When he zoomed in on it, he could see it had all the features of a squirrel, but he had never seen a squirrel that big and red in color. This would be something he hoped his father could explain to him. Yano had many questions for his parents and Sloppy to answer.

As he rode up to the house, he could see his father and Sloppy down at the barn. He removed the food supplies and returned them to the kitchen where his mother was cooking up a large pot of potato soup.

Odina hugged her son and told him she was glad he was home and wanted to hear all about his adventure when his father was there, so they could both hear it together.

Yano left the house to go to the barn to put Smokie in the pasture. He told his father and Sloppy that he had something amazing to tell them all about this adventure, but would wait until his mother could join them. Within ten minutes all of them were sitting around the table as Yano began to tell of his experience yesterday.

He started out telling how he rode down to the chair tree where they had seen the Wolf pups. "I climbed the same tree you did Father to get a better look at the cave opening and used the telescope for a while, but I never saw any critters there. I continued riding southwest and sensed something was watching me, but I didn't feel fear from being watched, I felt protected. I couldn't see anything watching me; it was just a feeling I had. Then, I rode over to the east side crossing over the trail to the cabin and found another cave at the bottom of a mountain with large boulders. I really wanted to explore the new cave that new cave I found, but remembered what you said to me about if I was injured to remember that I was all alone. Next time we go there, we can explore it together."

Alan smiled at his son and told him how proud he was of him.

"I went back to the cabin to fix supper and take care of Smokie. Laying on my bunk after supper, I thought of where I wanted to explore the next day. Something was telling me to go to the other side of the lake and explore that section of land. After breakfast the next morning, I left walking down to the southwest end of the lake to get to the other side. The land was mostly flat for about a hundred yards across to the next mountain. All of that land had large boulders everywhere, so I climbed up on top of one to get a better view. Using the telescope, I could see four deer going east, but the ghost deer wasn't with them. As I continued scanning the mountain side, movement caught my eyes on the west end of the mountain. Using the telescope, I found the movement, it was a squirrel jumping tree to tree as if it was frightened by something. With my naked eye, I noticed more movement down lower from where the squirrel was, so I used the telescope to see it better. I was amazed at what I was seeing. There were four half grown Wolves on the west end of the mountain close to the bottom. I had my elbows propped on my knees to hold the telescope steady as I watched them. Then one of the Wolves took a few steps in my direction, stopped and stared in my direction. The other three joined the first one and now I had four half grown Wolves staring in my direction. My elbow slipped off my knee, causing me to lose focus of them, when I propped my elbows on my knees again, the four Wolves were gone. I searched and searched that area with the telescope, but they were gone. Feeling sad that they were gone, I continued looking for them. As I sat still scanning that area, I felt a warm breath on my neck, and I slowly turned to my right. The warm breath I felt came from a very large Wolf that I was now nose to nose with. He looked deep into my eyes, as I was looking into his eyes. All of a sudden, this large Wolf put his head on my chest, and I placed my hands on the side of his head. I spoke in a calm voice and said, "WaYa."

The Wolf raised his head and stared deep into my soul. I then lowered my head and closed my eyes, and said, "I mean you no harm, I will protect you." When I raised my head and opened my eyes, the Wolf that I had touched and looked into his eyes was gone. I know he had been there, I touched him, I felt his breath on my neck, he looked into my eyes as I looked into his and now, he was gone. I knew I could find his tracks and the tracks of the other four, but they left no tracks. I could see my tracks and even found the tracks of the four deer, but the Wolves left no sign to see."

Alan, Odina and Sloppy were patiently listening to Yano's experience as he continued.

Yano said, "when I left that area to return to the cabin, I decided to explore more around the east end of the lake and also to look for Wolf tracks. Still no tracks were to be found. When I was back at the cabin cooking my supper, all I could think of was what I had seen and experienced just a few hours earlier." Yano said, "when I was finally able to fall asleep, I dreamed that the same large Wolf was sleeping on the floor beside my bunk. When I got up at daybreak, I looked at the floor, but the Wolf was not there." He said, "when I was packed up and headed home, I saw a critter that had red fur, that looked like a squirrel, but was twice as big as the gray squirrels I had seen and hunted."

Sloppy spoke up and said, "It was a fox squirrel that you saw, they are sometimes black in color and sometimes red."

Yano was content with Sloppy's answer about the squirrel, but then he asked, "what does it mean when I see the Wolves and am able to touch them, yet they leave no tracks?"

Odina looked at her son and said, "Yano, your family is Cherokee, and our tribal family is of the Wolf Clan. All of us in this room have heard the howling of the Wolf and understand it as being the Spirit of the Wolf, but none of us have ever seen a Wolf track. Only you and your father have seen the Wolf and only you have touched the Wolf. We all believe in The Spirit of the Wolf. The day you were born, the Wolf howled over my room where you were born. Your souls were connected and are meant to protect each other's spirit. Spirits leave no sign just like clouds leave no marks on the ground."

Alan spoke up and said, "That's right Son, you have been blessed by sharing the same soul of the Wolf."

Chapter 29

Sloppy was part of the Adams' family now and even though he went back to his place in the mountains often, he never stayed away more than two weeks at a time, then he would come out of the mountains and stay in the shanty Alan built for him. Sloppy had grown fond of the whole family, they had saved his life before and helped him in so many other ways.

Alan's Superintendent job at the coal mines in Rockford was going well and probably would be for the next fifteen years. He didn't think he would be there that long. Alan promised Mr. Stockburn that he would work two years at the new coal mine, then he might decide to leave and live off his land or find a job closer to town. He loved the coal mining business and appreciated getting the job and the promotions from Mr. Stockburn, but one hundred twenty miles a week for three days' work was getting tiring and it had him being away from his family a lot.

Odina loved her family, their little paradise and the life they had made there. She enjoyed teaching their children the Cherokee heritage and insisted that all of them get educated in the public school. She still made her Indian jewelry, and it was well known and requested from all over the state. She had even taught Ayita and Nokomis how to make jewelry, so they would have a trade to make money should they need it. All of the children were taught survival skills, how to live off the land if they should have to. The twins, Ayita and Koda were doing well in school and they had chores to do at home. Ayita's scar on her face had just about completely disappeared. Ayita's strength at seven years old, got her through that terrible time when the crazy man took her away from her family.

Nokomis, the baby girl, would start public school next year. Nokomis had been homeschooled by her mother all her young life. She spoke Cherokee as well as English. She enjoyed playing with her brothers and sister. They all rode their horses together with the older children always looking out for her. She had learned so much by helping her mother.

Yano was doing well in school and was responsible for the hard chores at home. He would soon be thirteen years old and had already done so much for a young man. Yano had gone on a few adventures by himself and survived for two or three days in the mountains. He loved adventures and exploring different sections of land. Yano helped search for his sister Ayita for three days when she was taken by a crazy man. He helped his father go to Sloppy's place only to find him near death and had to nurse him back to health enough to be brought back to their home to get medical treatment. On another adventure, he rode for two days by himself to find Sloppy's place in the mountains, so he could check on him. Sloppy was okay that time, but his horse had died, so Yano helped bury his horse, then let him ride his extra horse back to their home. Yano has been gifted with the Spirit of the Wolf in his soul.

Chapter 30

In 1847, Alan and Odina were married and in their first year, they lived in a little log cabin on his parents' land. Alan worked in the coal mines and Odina would make Indian jewelry to sell. They talked often of owning their own land and raising a family there. In 1848, Alan was told by some of his co-workers that a new mine was to open fifty miles north of High Point near the town of Shepherd Springs, Virginia and would be needing coal miners to work there. He also heard there were tracts of land there that could be purchased.

With hope, excitement and a little fear, they loaded their belongings and food supplies in their buckboard, hitched their two horses to it and headed north to chase their dream. They knew how to survive in the wilderness and to live off the land, if need be, for long periods of time.

They were able to sign a contract agreement on two hundred acres with a log cabin on it on their first day in Shepherd Springs, Virginia. They met a man who would be one of their best friends on their second day. Williard

Floyd, AKA, Sloppy was a true mountain man that lived in the Appalachian Mountains and only came out every few months for supplies. Other than the town merchants, their neighbors, the Bolins, were the next friends they met within their first few days of settling into their new place.

In the next thirteen years, Alan and Odina would have four amazing children. Yano was the first born, then the twins, Ayita and Koda and the fourth child was Nokomis. Two boys and two girls that loved to explore just like their parents. They taught their children the Cherokee language and heritage, so they could pass it on to their children. Their little paradise has grown to one thousand acres and many treasures had been found. They had found gold, precious gemstones, Ginseng plants, wild game and fish for food, but their most precious treasures were their friends.

Alan had worked for Stockburn Mining Company for thirteen years and is now the Superintendent of the Stockburn coal mines in Rockford, Virginia. He has to travel by train sixty miles north of Shepherd Springs to oversee the mining operations three days a week while his family remains in Shepherd Springs. There have been some tragic events with their friends. Their neighbor, Clyde Bolin had his leg and ankle broken by a large hog; he then got pneumonia. They were going to lose their farm due to missed payments, so Alan and Odina were able to help, so they could keep their farm.

Alan and Yano found Sloppy near death at his cabin deep in the Appalachian Mountains. Sloppy would always stop by when he came out of the mountains, and Alan was worried since he had not seen him in months, so he and Yano went on an adventure to find his place and check on him. It's a good thing they did, they saved his life.

The worst evil experience was when Alan and Odin's seven-year-old daughter, Ayita, was taken by a crazy man. Sloppy and Yano started the search for Ayita. A telegram was sent to Rockford to advise Alan that his daughter had been taken. Within the next sixteen hours, there were eight men on the search including her father, Alan. Alan was alone when he found his daughter with the crazy man, three days later. The crazy man had burned a scar on her face with a hot knife blade, he had the same scar on his face. When Alan ordered him to put his gun down, he pointed it at Alan. Alan fired his first shot, and the crazy man would never again harm another child. Sloppy was part of the Adams' family now and would always stay with them when he came out of the mountains to get supplies.

As told by the Cherokee elders, the location of the howling Wolf is where treasures can be found, but they may not always be gold or gemstones. Treasures could mean anything of value or purpose. In 1846, Sloppy found his best friend that had been missing for four days dead at the location of the howling Wolf. Alan found a treasure of buried gold at the location of the howling Wolf. When Yano was being born, a vision of the howling Wolf was directly over the room he was born in.

When Yano was ten years old, he told his father, he thought he was already a man because he could track and hunt for food and was good at doing chores.

His father told him he could give him a test to see if he was ready for the journey into manhood.

When Yano was sitting on a stump up in the mountains all night blindfolded and by himself, he heard the howling of the Wolf. After daylight, he removed his blindfold and saw his father sitting behind him. He had been keeping a watch over his brave young son all night. He was Yano's treasure.

Then there was the time when Alan was about to be attacked by a mountain lion until he heard the howling of the Wolf, then saw the image of the Wolf just above him on the rock cliff that scared the big cat away.

Yano found some gold nuggets at a location where he heard the howling of the Wolf then a little later, he saw what he believed to be four Wolf pups. A few months later, Yano was on one of his adventures where he saw four Wolves a little over a hundred yards away, then as he turned to his right, he was nose to nose with a very large Wolf. He was not frightened; the Wolf was not aggressive and put his head against Yano's chest. Yano held the Wolf's head with his hands. Yano has been given the gift of having the Spirit of the Wolf in his soul.

He had heard the howling of the Wolf, he had seen the Wolves, and he had touched the Wolf and yet, they left no signs. No one that has heard the Wolf howl or seen images of the Wolf has ever seen any tracks of the Wolf.

Sloppy spends most of his time staying with the Adams in a shanty they built for him. He only goes to his mountain place every couple of months and only stays there about two weeks at the time. He knows if he stays longer, Yano or Alan will make the two-day ride to check on him. He still loves the mountain life, but he is getting older and that makes it harder to do what he used to do there.

Alan and Yano have enlarged the little cabin at the lake. Now the whole family can go there and spend a few days enjoying the lake and exploring the land. They can even pan for gold together, teaching the younger children what to look for and how to keep secrets on what and where they find treasure.

Yano continues to go on his adventures when he can. Learning more about surviving the mountain life every time he goes.

Living in the Appalachian Mountains can be difficult if you don't love it, but the Adams truly love it and just their way of life.

The Spirit of the Wolf exists in this mountain range and is thought of being the protectors for the people that live here.

229

The End January 17,2024